# Cut N' Curl

# Rayven Skyy

Follow me on Twitter @ Rayven_Skyy

ISBN-13:
978-1482049626
ISBN-10:
1482049627

# ACKNOWLEDGEMENTS

I have to give praises to my Lord and Savior for the many blessings He bestows on me every second of my life.

I'm going to make this short, and sweet so y'all can get to what you paid for—Cut N' Curl! I want to thank you all soooooooooooo much for rocking with me for as long as you have. The support I receive from you all is truly a blessing. To my editor Shannon Fields, I love and appreciate you. My faithful assistant, Shantelle Brown, I am truly thankful to have you on my team! Stesha Manning *salute* (Inside joke y'all) you know what's up! To the admins of the Rayven Skyy Fan Club on Facebook, I'kia and Tonikia, I really appreciate you ladies taking the time to start the group, and I promise we will get some more discussions in soon. To everyone who has liked my Fan Page on FB, to anyone who has ever downloaded a Rayven Skyy book, to those that post reviews giving me the good and the bad, I really appreciate it to the upmost! Special shout out to my FB buddy Farryn Grant who keeps me well entertained.To fellow authors, Aaron Bebo, Solea Dehvine, Shareef Jaudon, Maurice "First" Tonia, and a host of others, I wish you all much continued success in this writing game.

Rayven

# Dedication

This one goes to my baby, daughter, proofreader and friend, Saysha Sandra-Janea Wood. She fell in love with Juju's character in Another Rumble, and literally begged me to write a book about him. Thank you for being so understanding and cooking a few meals when your momma is locked up in her bedroom for hours on end, banging on the keyboards. We may not always see eye-to-eye, but just know I will always have your back! I love you.

# Cut N' Curl

## Rayven Skyy

# Say What I Mean!

I pulled into my designated parking space in front of Cut N' Curl, and turned off the ignition. I looked around to see if everyone was still here waiting for me as I had instructed them to do and to my surprise; they were . . . Umm . . . hmmm—clears throat—I meant to say, they better still be here. I've got to get a few things in order now that I am the proud owner of Cut N' Curl, and I refuse to put up with all the foolishness Lea allowed to take place in the salon on a daily basis —not Juju!

I adjusted the rearview mirror to get one last glimpse of myself before exiting my car.

"Muah!" I blew myself a kiss in the rearview mirror. "The lip-gloss is popping!" I rubbed my lips together to evenly distribute the shine. "Get it bitch!" I smiled. "Come on here Whitney."

Oh, where are my manners? Let me introduce you all to my pride and joy; my baby Whitney. Mike—my boyfriend of three years—bought Whitney for me after I suffered a devastating loss earlier this year. I will never forget where I was the day Whitney Houston passed away. Oh, how I was beside myself that day and I'm sure many of you were as well. I couldn't eat or sleep, let alone get out of the bed. I've been Whitney Houston's

1

biggest fan since the day she graced the stage at the tender age of eighteen. I remember when I used to steal my mother's lip-stick and wrap t-shirts around my head pretending I had long luxurious hair as I crooned along with Whitney to her classic song, *How Will I Know* in the mirror for hours on end. Oh, how I loved her so. There will never be another "true" Diva like Whitney—fuck what you heard!

As my way of paying homage to the "Queen of Pop" I named my Bichon Frise after her. My Whitney stands approximately twelve inches tall, roughly weighing ten pounds, and she has the most beautiful snow-white coat which requires very little maintenance even though I brush her hair for at least ten to fifteen minutes a day. It helps to keep it fluffy and tamed. About every six weeks I scissor the most unique hair-styles in her hair and now Whitney is rocking a fierce Mohawk.

I take her with me everywhere I go because that's what a "good mother" does. I've realized that this may be the closest I will ever get to parenthood and that's fine by me. As busy as I am with the salon, and with Mike's demanding job as a teacher, we don't have time to be full-time parents anyway.

Not too many things have changed since the salon changed hands other than Precious and Regina's sudden departure which actually saved me the grueling task of firing the lazy jealous bitches! Precious seemed to have a problem with telling time and she never showed up for work until well after noon, whereas, Regina didn't make a move without Precious' consent. Honestly, I do believe them two bitches shared the same brain. I sure hope they did not think they were hurting my feelings when they both quit once I purchased Cut N' Curl. Fuck 'em and feed 'em fish—is what I say.

Nicole's trifling ass is no longer with us either after she got caught getting her *Wynona Rider* on— that's stealing for those of you who can't keep up—in Macy's Department store in MacArthur Mall, and ain't nobody heard from the jealous bitch since then. Not even Milk, according to Sabrina.

Janea still works at the shop—I know you remember her shameful ass, don't you?—and yes "dick" is still her conversation piece of choice. And then there's Angelle—she still can't dress worth a damn, but a Sweetie Pie nonetheless—who ain't been right since her baby daddy—and sometimes boyfriend when he wasn't in prison— Onion was found with his throat sliced from ear-to-ear a few years ago. Each day was a mystery as to which one of her personalities was going to show up to work. I think Angelle is still trying to figure out where do broken hearts go.

And lastly—as well as to the very least—there's Kabo, whom is also the one giving me the greatest resistance at this point. Kabo and I haven't been able to get along since the day he set up shop in Cut N' Curl, and we can't seem to set horses now. Lea hired him with the hopes of bringing new patrons to the shop, but if you ask me his presence has only brought the moral in the shop down to an all-time low, and as of recent he has taken his rebellion toward me to extreme heights; but all that shit is about to change!

I scooped Whitney up and nestled her tightly under my left arm and then reached for the cane that was lying across the backseat. I clicked the lock button on my key ring once I was out the car and walked toward the salon. They must be waiting for me in the backroom—also per my instructions—because I didn't see any lights on as I approached the front door. You see what I'm talking about? They know Juju don't play; I say what I mean, and mean what I say!

Once I reached the front door, I looked down one last time to ensure everything was in place as far as the outfit I had chosen specifically for tonight's meeting was concerned. I'm a business man now and I thought it best that I tone down the bright colors and what not. Instead, I opted for a more business casual appearance while I'm at work performing my managerial duties, but I still rock my heels on my off days. Tonight, I deemed my black, long-sleeved Ralph Lauren button-up shirt, and dark Michael Kors slacks, accented with my black-and-white Stacy Adams—circa 1997, limited edition—platform shoes were most fitting. If you are going to be the boss you have to look the part!

I eagerly inserted my key into the lock ready to make my grand entrance when I noticed that the door was slightly ajar.

*"Umph! What if I was a rapist or a serial killer? All of their asses would be dead!"* I thought to myself. You see this shit? This is the bullshit I was speaking of earlier. I swiftly kicked the door completely open as if I were Clint Eastwood, and immediately slammed it shut.

"Can anybody tell me," I shouted, as I headed toward the backroom, "why the hell this front door is laying wide open?" I paused for an explanation. They couldn't have heard me because I wasn't acknowledged with so much as a head nod.

Whitney and I had rehearsed how we would make our arrival to the meeting several times before we left the house and this was not what I had envisioned. I was supposed to be led into the room by Whitney on a leash for theatrical effects. *'Oh, well; so much for that.'* I politely cleared my throat and simply repeated myself.

"I said, can anybody tell me why this front door is laying wide open when the shop is closed for business?" Janea briefly exchanged eye contact with me for a fraction of a second and then continued to eat her Chinese food. "Anybody could have walked in here on y'all!" I raised my voice. "Do y'all not watch The First 48, or Tru TV?" I looked at them one-by-one. "Huh?"

"Man, don't nobody want to hear all that shit!" Kabo stood up and tossed the magazine he was reading down on the make-shift table centered in the middle of the floor that consisted of two end tables pushed together. A one of a kind design by yours truly. "What the hell did you call this meeting for? I started to say fuck it and 'head on home. I got shit to do, plus my old lady waiting on me." Just the sound of his voice made me furious!

"Did you just interrupt me, Cujo?" I pointed at him with my cane.

"My name is mothafuckin' Kabo! How many times do I have to tell yo' ass that, Sugar Daddy?" Angelle interrupted our exchange of words with a sigh.

"Juju, can you just tell us what you called this meeting for? My girls are at home waiting for me, too." Kabo sat back down.

I took a deep breath and let out a sigh of my own. I lowered Whitney down to the floor, attached the leash to her collar, and then walked her around the table as I stared at them individually with my other hand behind my back.

"Very well, then." I circled around the table. "Now that you've taken your seats, I will adjourn the meeting." Angelle and Kabo simultaneously looked at one another and then broke out into laughter. "What the hell is so funny?"

"Man, come on with this bullshit!" Kabo was now on his feet again. "Talking 'bout, you will adjourn the meeting." He tapped Angelle on her arm. "That's what the fuck you do when the meeting is over, Tasty Kake!" he continued to laugh. *'That's it!'*

"Sit yo' jealous bitch ass down before I make a dollar out of fifteen cents!" I yelled, erupting into my best Nino Brown voice with my cane extended in Kabo's face.

Food went flying out of Janea's mouth and she too joined in on the laughter. Now I know how Nino felt in *New Jack City* when his subordinates were disobedient. I watched the movie on BET earlier today and I told myself that's who I needed to channel while conducting tonight's meeting— Nino Brown!

"Boy, you know yousa' fool!" Janea declared, as she patted her chest to keep from choking on the remaining food in her mouth. "Juju are you serious?"

I lowered my cane and placed it up against the wall. I unhooked Whitney's leash so she could roam freely and then reached inside of my bag to retrieve the gavel I purchased from Office Max yesterday.

*Tap . . . tap . . . tap . . .* I banged the gavel down on the table and cleared my throat once again.

"Hear ye' . . . hear ye' . . . hear ye'. This meeting is now called to order." I looked around the room. "When I call your name just simply state that you are present. Taco?" I eyed Kabo.

"Present, Sweet Cheeks," he answered.

"Angellllle?" I curled my tongue putting emphasize on the *"elle"* at the ending of her name.

"Juju?" Angelle eye-balled me with flaring nostrils.

"Girl, just say you present." Janea encouraged. "And before you call my name, I'm present, too," she included.

"Very, well. One of the first items I wish to address and make as clear as my lip-gloss is that when I talk," I gently placed my right hand on my chest, "you people listen. If the chair does not recognize you or until I convey to you that you have the floor you shall remain silent!" I immediately turned my head toward Kabo and shot him an intense wide—eye Tyra Banks look while batting my eye lashes. The room fell silent for a split second, but then a roar of laughter filled the air once again.

"Man, I'm gone!" Kabo said, and walked toward the back door. Janea was laughing so hard she had tears coming out her eyes.

"Get him Whitney," I commanded. "Bite his ass!"

"I wish that mutt would come over here so I can kick the shit out of him," Kabo replied angrily.

"And I wish the fuck you would kick my got damn baby." I reached for my cane. "Yo' ass gon' be spending the night in 811 for animal cruelty!" I informed Kabo, referring to the Norfolk City Jail's address. "Right after I beat the fuck out of you with this stick!" *For real I was going to need more than a stick for this big nigga but Juju ain't never scared.'*

"I ain't never liked yo' ass anyway, you ugly motherfucka'!"

"Kiss my ass Fruit Loops!" Kabo spluttered, as he walked out the back door.

"This is utterly ridiculous," Angelle said.

"I'm surprised at you two." I squinted my eyes, as I pointed at them with my cane. "Y'all are supposed to be my bitches. I've known you two whores longer than you've known Kabo." I slumped down in the chair Kabo once occupied. "Y'all are always taking his side." I rolled my eyes and crossed my legs. *'Fuck all of them!'*

"Taking his side how, Juju?" Janea got up to throw the empty plastic bowl into the trash can. "Why, 'cause we're laughing at your silly ass?" She reached inside of the mini-refrigerator and took out a can soda.

"Yes! Where's the loyalty?" I made a sour face as I sat up in the chair. Janea was trying, unsuccessfully, to control her laughter, but as soon as she would look in my direction the giggling started again. *'I can't stand these jealous bitches!'*

"Look Juju, just because you own the shop now doesn't mean that you have to start acting like you're running a salon boot camp. We all know who we pay booth rent to, and we have a clear understanding as to whom the HBIC is up in here." She winked. "You!"

I relaxed my shoulders and rested my back up against the chair. Finally, some respect!

"Thank you for saying that Janea," I replied, adjusting my attitude toward her. Clearly, she has seen the error of her ways. "I really do appreciate it. I don't mean to come down hard on you people, but it can be a difficult task transitioning from an employee to the boss. I'm sure you can understand where I'm coming from." I was now speaking in my corporate voice.

"Yes Juju, we understand," she sneered. "Any other rules you care to share with us tonight?" she asked in a sarcastic tone. *'Oh, this bitch is trying to carry me.'*

"I see Janea that you seem to think that you're smarter than a fifth grader," I said, acknowledging the fact that I was on to her clowning. "And you almost had me but I'm going to beat this salon into shape one way or another. And for all who don't like it either move on or get pissed on!"

"It's your world and I'm just a squirrel." Janea stood up. Angelle got up, too, and put her purse on her shoulder.

"Janea, can you give me a ride home?"

"Yeah, come on." They were both about to follow Kabo's injurious example—meaning fucked up!—and leave out the back door when Janea stopped and turned around. "Oh my bad Juju, is the meeting adjourned?"

*'Oh now she's really fucking with me.'*

"I don't have anything else to say to you two jealous bitches!"

"We love you, too, Juju," Janea said before walking out the door.

"Come on, Whitney," I summoned her. "Let's go."

# Fuck-a-licous!

"Girl I'm going to start looking for me another shop to work at." Angelle slammed the passenger side door shut. "Juju is really starting to get on my fucking nerves!"

"Damn, you mad ain't cha'?" I looked over at Angelle as I fastened the seat belt. "Juju got you cussing and slamming doors. I know you mad, but bitch don't slam my door like that again or your ass gon' walk."

I started up the car and pulled off.

"For real, Janea?" Angelle looked at me annoyingly. "Nino Brown?" I started laughing again thinking about Juju's crazy ass. "I might've taken him a little more seriously had he came up in there with a British accent professing to be Tabitha from Tabitha's Salon Takeover, but Nino Brown? Girl I ain't got time for that shit."

"Juju must've really gotchu' hot," I teased her. "That's two cuss words in less than two minutes." I prodded Angelle on her shoulder.

"I'm serious Janea. It doesn't bother you?"

"Hell to-the-fucking nawl! You keep allowing Juju to rent space in your brain. His ass will calm down once the newness of the shop wears off," I told her. "Where is your car anyway, Angelle?"

"Shantelle had to work late tonight so I let her drop me off today."

"And where is that hot ass Rochelle," I asked, referring to Shantelle's twin sister.

"Who knows? I haven't seen her in three days." She turned her head toward the window.

"Three days?" I glanced over at Angelle after stopping at the red light. "She hasn't called or anything?"

"Go." She nodded her head forward.

"What?"

"The light is green, Janea." I took my foot off of the brake and pressed down on the gas pedal. "And I don't feel like talking about Rochelle right now."

"I told you what you need to do for Rochelle. Cuff her ass up by her collar," I balled my hand up into a fist, "and fuck her up one good time. I guarantee you won't have any more problems out of her." I turned the windshield wipers on because it had started to drizzle.

"That girl is as tall as me and she is too old to be getting beatings. Plus, I'm tired of arguing with her. Rochelle is just going to have to find out the hard way," she said, as she fidgeted with her finger nails.

"Yep, and the hard way would be my fist straight to that shit up under her nose, her mouth!"

"Where are you on your way to anyway?" I knew she was just trying to change the subject.

"Harry O's after I drop you off," I answered. One good thing Juju has done since taking over Cut N' Curl was installing a shower in the bathroom, which saved me the trouble of having to go all the way home after work when I made plans for the evening, but we could have done without the mural he had painted on the wall of him and Whitney donned in matching outfits.

"Janea, do you ever get tired of hanging out?"

"Nope," I quickly answered. "I don't have no kids and I'm single and always ready to mingle, so what's the problem? You need to get your ass out the house and have some fun for a change and stop letting Rochelle drive you crazy."

"There ain't anything in the club I want to see," she chided with disdain.

"Harry O's isn't really a club Angelle, it's more like a bar and grill. Either way you still need to get out the house. Go to the movies, go get you a pedicure or better yet have a spa day. You work your fingers to the bones to maintain your household so treat yourself sometimes."

"I'm saving money to buy the twins a car," she explained.

"Now Shantelle does deserve a car of her own because she will work," I praised her youngest daughter. "But that damn Rochelle," I shook my head, "I wouldn't buy her a bike with training wheels with her lazy ass. She needs to get out there and find her a job, too."

"Janea?" Angelle folded her arms across her chest and sighed.

"I wouldn't care if it was picking hair out of a bear's ass at least it's a job. You gon' kill your damn-self trying to pay your bills and keep her dolled up, too. Does she have Boom-Boom with her?" I asked, referring to Rochelle's two-year-old son.

"You know what?" She unfastened her seat belt. "I'm getting sick and tired of people telling me how to raise my girls. Unless I ask you for your advice please keep it to yourself." I glanced over at Angelle long enough to see her roll her eyes.

"Only because I've known you for almost ten years I'mma' let you have that one but the next time Rochelle jumps at you, on top of you, in front of you, or beside you, don't call me!"

After I dropped Angelle off at home I headed back down Rosemont Road toward Lynnhaven Parkway to Harry O's. It was Karaoke night and I couldn't wait to see who would be up in the building tonight. Juju used to hang out with me after work on Friday nights before he bought Cut N' Curl, and Harry O's would be the first spot we'd hit, but I seem to be beneath him at the present moment.

Juju is funny as shit, ain't he? You know how people with new money can perform, don't you? Yeah . . . like they ain't never had shit! He just has his ass on his shoulders right now. I give it a few more weeks then he'll be back to his normal self.

Juju has exceptional clientele, and he can really fuck with some hair, but he also has champagne taste with bulging beer pockets with all that he is trying to achieve. I'm not saying there's anything wrong with upgrading the salon but he's trying to do too much, too soon.

Juju and Mike just bought a house less than two years ago, and he also recently traded in the car Mike bought for him in for a brand new Cadillac Escalade, then Juju had the Cut N' Curl logo tinted on the truck to exhibit to all the jealous bitches—as only he can say—out in the world that he had arrived. I think the shit is funny for real, and Angelle ain't the only one working her fingers to the bone. Shit is so tight for Juju right now he opened the shop up on Sunday, which was right up Angelle's alley. There were two stylists that left the shop after it changed hands and they both benefited from their departure by picking up new clientele. Me and Kabo got a bet going on between us as to which one out of the two will crash and burn first, and I have my money waged against Angelle.

I told Angelle to sell the house Onion bought for them right before he died but Angelle refuses to. I know her mortgage has to be at least three grand a month—give or take—and when you factor in the note for her BMW —another gift from Onion—I'm for certain she's hardly making ends meet. I also suggested to Angelle that she trade her car in for something less expensive but she won't do that either. I know the only reason she insisted Onion buy her that damn BMW in the first place was to keep up with what Nicole was doing. The pair had become the best of friends, unbeknownst to Angelle, that Nicole was fucking her man. And folks talk about me!

Yeah, I still like to fuck with no shame about it. I have a substantial clientele listing myself and I pay my own bills, take care of my grandma, and I don't bother a soul. I could give two fucks what anyone has to say about me; because I'mma' do Janea. I've come to the conclusion that life is a party that I am invited to everyday and I plan on living mines to the fullest. So, if I meet somebody that I want to fuck, I'm grown, he's grown, so what's the problem? And to quote the late Billie Holiday, "It *'taint* nobody's business if I do!"

Since I've talked about everyone in the shop I might as well throw in my two-cents regarding Kabo, too. You'd think he would be used to Juju by now since he has been doing Talisha's—Kabo's fiancé—hair for several years now, but to say he can't stand Juju is an understatement. If you ask me Kabo is just homophobic. Ever since he started working at Cut N' Curl, even before Lea sold the shop, not a day has passed since that Kabo hasn't insulted Juju in some sort of fashion.

I pushed up on Kabo when he first came to the shop—you know how I do—but I figured Talisha had him pussy whipped because my advances were ignored. All I can say is baby-girl best to keep that tight leash around his neck; with his sexy chocolaty ass! All he has to do is say the word and Kabo is as good as fucked.

I could tell from the number of cars parked outside Harry O's when I pulled up there was a nice crowd inside tonight. I sprayed a little perfume behind each ear and a few squirts in between my legs before I got out to the car. I pulled down my dress that had crept up my thighs while I was driving, and closed the door behind me. I'm so proud of the way I've been able to maintain my weight loss since my surgery and I pray to God I'm not wasting a cute outfit on a bunch of "Hood Boogers" tonight.

"Janea," a voice hollered out my name. I turned around to see who it was, but I never stopped walking toward the entrance of the bar.

"Who is that?" I hollered back. I reached into my purse in search of my mace. You never can be too safe.

"Girl, come here. This yo' cousin," he shot back. I stood on the sidewalk and waited for him to catch up with me now that I knew who it was. "You ain't see me flashing my lights at you?" Tyke asked, as he walked toward me.

"Naw I ain't see you." I reached out to give him a hug. "Whatchu' doing up here anyway? Why you ain't at Royale Blue with the rest of the youngins'?" I teased him.

Royale Blue was a night club, also in Virginia Beach, that catered to a younger crowd. I've been to Royale Blue a few times when it first opened, but it wasn't my cup of tea. I don't do "Gerber Dick." Just in case I lost you, Gerber is baby food and anything under the age of twenty-five was too young for me. They're dick game has yet to fully mature, and they fuck like Jack rabbits, so why waste my time? I have a lot of different terminology for classifying dick so remember where you heard it first.

"Don't hate 'cause you an old head," Tyke countered my sarcasm.

"Who's that with you, Tyke?" I nodded my head at the light-skinned guy walking toward us.

"That's my nigga Terrell. He just came home a few months ago. I don't think you know him. He was locked up when you and Grandma moved down here."

"He got a woman?" I grinned at my cousin.

"Shit, I don't know. Ask him yo' damn self. Yo' man, this my cousin Janea," Tyke introduced us to one another.

"Terrell." he reached out his hand to me.

"It's nice to meet you, Terrell." I continued to smile. "You have some pretty eyes, you know that?"

"Girl, boo!" My cousin walked in between us and broke up our hand lock. "Bring yo' ass on here."

As we approached the entrance to Harry O's, Terrell leaped in front to open the door for me. Once inside Terrell told the cashier stationed on the other side of the door that he was paying the cover charge for all three of us. Tyke announced that he was going to use the bathroom after ordering himself a drink. When he returned he then made his way over to where the pool table was positioned in another room within the bar, leaving me and Terrell alone.

Karaoke was already under way and Alicia Key's song, *I'm Ready* was being serenaded to the patrons by last week's winner. Terrell sat down in a bar stool to the left of me. The waitress called him by his name and asked if he wanted to start another tab. He told her that he did, and he gave her several hundred dollar bills to cover his tab from the night before. Terrell then handed her another two-hundred dollars to pay for his drinks tonight. *'Damn; is he an alcoholic?'* I need to assess this situation before I put him on the "Nu-Nu" list.

What is "Nu-Nu" you ask? In laymen terms it means new dick. Don't get me wrong; I love drunk dick, too, but not *sloppy* drunk dick! Men tend to get heavier when they're sloppy drunk, and then they turn into lazy participants when the time comes to fuck. Sloppy drunk niggas aren't able to support their own body weight, and they can never locate your pussy unassisted. They're sloppy when it comes to kissing, they sweat their asses off, and not only do you get a salt shower; they fuck you horribly, too. *'I might have to put the duck on this one.'*

"I like your dress Janea," Terrell complimented me. "You're wearing that shit girl." He passed me a drink.

"Thank you. What is this?" I took a sip.

"Coconut Ciroc with pineapple juice. Shit good ain't it?" He raised up his glass.

"It is." I nodded my head in approval. "You don' turned me on to something."

"You want something to eat," he asked. I hate when niggas ask me that. I could see if I was still plus-sized, but I'm down to a size nine now. *'Do I look hungry?'*

"Naw, sweetie, I'm good." I took another sip of my drink.

"She's good," Terrell said, signaling to the girl on stage.

"She a'ight," I challenged.

"Whatchu' mean, *'she' a'ight'*?" he mocked. "Shorty can blow."

"If she got her breathing under control she could hold her high notes a little longer."

"Is that right?" He sat his drink down.

As I viewed Terrell's side profile, I noticed a scar on the side of his face. His light-skin made it more visible even though the lights were dim. I could tell the scar had some years on it and I'm sure a story behind it, too. I reached over and ran my fingers across the side of his face. There was something sensual, as well as mysterious about his scar that intrigued me. Terrell's hazel eyes, coupled with his muscular body, definitely catapulted him into the "Fuck-a-licous" category.

"Like I said . . . she a'ight," I repeated.

"So, I guess you could do better?" Terrell rubbed the back of my hand. I answered his dare with a melody.

*"I was wondering maybe . . . could I make you my baby . . . if we do the unthinkable . . . would that make us look crazy . . ."* Terrell responded with a verse of his own.

*"Or would it be so beautiful . . . either way I'm saying . . ."* I joined in to complete the last verse. *"If you ask me I'm ready . . ."*

"I know that's right!" I smiled at him. I'm a good singer but Terrell has me beat. *'Uuummm . . . Fuck-a-licous with a cherry on top!'* "You ready to go up there and do a duet with me?"

"Naw," Terrell shook his head. "I'm more of a shower singer. You go 'head."

"Not with vocal cords like that."

"Stop trying to fill me up with octane Janea." He laughed.

"No, I'm serious Terrell. You have a very nice voice," I assured him. "No bullshit."

"Where yo' man at, Janea?"

"At home with his wife," I winked at him. "Can I get another drink?"

"Yeah," he said, and told the bartender to give us both another round. "So that means you coming home with me tonight, right?"

"It's too soon to tell," I answered, playing hard to get. "But if you sing to me again I'll definitely think about it." I smiled at him seductively.

"Is that right?"

"Oh, that's so right!"

Terrell leaned down close to my ear.

*"Girl I promise . . . you won't regret it . . . and everything that you've ever wanted . . .I'mma' strip to the bone and just let you get on it girl . . ."*

Damn . . . he sung that shit better than R. Kelly did and he wrote it. *Ummm* . . . Fuck-a-licous with a cherry on top and whipped cream! I'll holler at y'all later.

# Pressing Matters!

Do you see the bullshit I have to contend with? That fucking Kabo is something else, and if he thinks he's going to get away with disrupting my meeting tonight he has another thing coming. I'm Julius "Mothafuckin' Juju" Wright, and I am not easily broken. It's either going to be my way or the fucking highway!

Speaking of highway, this got damn Portsmouth Tunnel is backed the fuck up again. Shit! That's the only thing I hate about living in the Churchland area. I guess neither Mike, nor I, took into consideration the fact that we would have to commute via the tunnel to get back and forth to work when purchasing our first home. This shit is truly in the mothafuckin' way, and after forty-five minutes of bumper-to-bumper traffic, Whitney and I finally made our way to our humble abode.

"Look at this shit, Whitney. Mike got every damn light on in this mothafucka'. It's no wonder the damn light bill is sky high. I guess yo' papi is afraid the Boogie Man is gon' get him." As we approached the front door I could see that it was open. *'What the fuck is wrong with people not locking damn doors?'* "Mike?" I closed the door behind me once we were inside and locked it. I put

Whitney down and she quickly ran off toward the kitchen. "Will you look at this shit, Mike?"

"I'm upstairs, babe."

"Now you know this don't make no got damn sense," I said to myself, as I looked around the house. "Mike!"

"Why are you hollering like that?"

"No, the question is why do you have yo' funky ass shoes and socks sprawled up and down the stairs? Who the fuck do I look like to you, Benson?" I said, as I approached the top of the stairs. "And furthermore, why was the front door laying wide open? You're worse than them fools at the shop. Anybody could be in this house right now and you would never know it."

"And hello to you, too," he replied, attempting to be funny.

"Got this damn hallway smelling like funky ass Fritos Corn Chips. I'm not no damn maid and I'm not going to keep picking up behind you!" I threw his shoes and socks in the middle of our bedroom floor.

"How did the meeting go, babe?" Mike bent down to pick up his belongings off the floor.

"Like shit!" I flopped down on the bed.

"What happened?" He threw his shoes into the closet and put his socks in the dirty clothes basket.

"That fucking' Kabo as usual." I jerked my neck. "That sorry sack of shit should be throwing rose pedals in front of me when I walk. Had it not been for me he would have never met Talisha," I ranted.

"What did he do this time, Juju?" Mike sat down on the bed beside me.

"I really don't want to talk about it right now," I sulked.

"Well, don't let that ruin the rest of your night," he kissed me on the cheek. "I have some papers to grade before morning so-"

"Yeah . . . yeah . . . yeah . . ." I waved my hand in the air. I had officially tuned Mike out at this point. I had other pressing matters on my mind right now to deal with.

# Drag Queen Antics!

I opened the door to my apartment, sat my bag down on the living room table, and headed straight for the kitchen.

"Talisha?" I called out to my fiancé, as I rummaged through the refrigerator in search of something quick to eat. "Baby, where you at?" I hollered. My eyes scanned each shelf one by one. *'When the fuck is she gon' go grocery shopping?'*

"I'm right here," she answered.

"I see you ain't cook nothing tonight, again!" I crumpled up my face and slammed the refrigerator door. *'A nigga would die from miss-meal cramps 'round this mothafucka' waiting on Talisha to cook a meal.'*

"Well, maybe you can get you a hot meal over at James' house," she shouted, crossing her arms. She must've been going through my cell phone again. I was rushing when I left out of the house this morning and forgot it. "Kabo, you might want to step your player game up just a tad bit. Putting bitches numbers in your cell phone under a dude's name has to be one of the oldest tricks in the handbook. You mean to tell me that with all this new technology out here y'all niggas ain't figured out a better system yet to hide your shit?"

"That is James' phone number, Talisha. You called it didn't you? Shit, what I ask you that for I know you did." I instantly created a note in my mental rolodex to put the number under a different name.

"Yeah, I called it and some bitch name Cheryl answered the phone," she retorted.

"Cheryl is his wife Talisha and I just started cutting his hair." I shook my head at her. "Stay the hell out of my phone please. I don't go through your cell phone do I?"

"I'm telling you Kabo," she put her right hand up in a stop position, "if I find out that you're cheating on me with some bitch the wedding is off. I don't care how much money we've spent on it!" she protested.

"Talisha ain't nobody cheating with no bitches. I told you I cut the nigga hair. I got one bitch and you the only bitch I need." I quickly moved away from the swing that was headed in my direction and when she missed her intended target—me—we both started laughing.

"Who the fuck is you calling a bitch, Kabo?" she asked in the midst of our amusement. Talisha knew I was just joking with her. I would never call her a bitch. Well, not to her face I wouldn't. I scooped her up into a tight embrace and embedded kisses all over her neck. "Owww . . . you're hurting me Kabo," she moaned. I worked out on the regular and sometimes I handled Talisha's petite 5'6 frame a little too rough.

"Look." I put her down and grabbed her by the hand. "When I asked you to marry me I thought we were passed all this bullshit."

"We are, baby." She kissed me on the lips. "I'm sorry. I promise I won't do it again." I wrinkled up my lips and looked at her side-ways.

"Ummm . . . hmmm . . . instead of being in here all in my shit violating my privacy, you should've had yo' ass in this kitchen getting yo' Rachael Ray on. I'm hungry as a mothafucka'. What we eating tonight?"

"Let's go out somewhere to eat," she suggested, which was her usual proposal. Talisha never liked to cook.

"I told you we're not going out to eat every damn night and pay for this wedding, too. Its gon' be one or the other. Do you know how many mothafuckin' heads I got to cut to pay for that thousand dollar cake you picked out? Shit, no sooner than I make the money yo' ass don' spent it."

"Kabo, don't act like you're the only one who is paying for this wedding. I have made some major sacrifices in order to pay for this wedding too, nigga!" She placed both hands on her hips.

*'I never understood why y'all women do that silly shit, putting your hands on your hips. Does that help y'all get your point across better?'*

"Like what? What have you paid for, Talisha?" I put my hands on my hips imitating her current stance.

29

"You need to stop doing that." She laughed, and then lowered her hands.

"Doing what?" I laughed, too.

"Pretending to be gay," she smirked. "You look a little too natural doing it."

"That comes from being 'round that punk ass Julia all day at the shop," I said, referring to Juju. I opened the refrigerator door again to see what I could put together to eat. It looks like I'm on my own tonight as far as dinner was concerned.

"Stop talking about my hair stylist," she said in a whiney voice. "Why are you always being mean to him, Kabo?"

"Fuck Juju! I hate to see a man parade around like a bitch, that's why." I decided on a ham-and-turkey wrap that I had left over from the night before and a bag of Lay's potato chips.

"You act like you've never been around gay people before," she said, as she climbed up on a bar stool to continue our weekly debate about all the reasons I detest Juju.

"I don't have a problem with him being gay but still be a man with yo' shit. I understand why you like him so much though, you give the faggot enough of my money getting your hair fixed every damn week. Besides, you two have a lot more in common with each other than I do." I pulled out the bar stool and sat my food down on the table.

"What do you mean we have a lot in common?" she asked, reaching for my bag of chips.

"Aught!" I tapped the back of her hand. "Get back!" I sat down. "But, what grown man walks around in high heeled shoes with his toes freshly painted and shit?"

"You talk all the shit you want to about Juju but he keeps himself up better than most women I know. You could learn a thing or two from him style wise anyway."

"The fuck I can," I said, as I chewed my food.

"Stop talking with your mouth full." Talisha hit me upside my head as if she were my mother. "And did you give Juju his wedding invitation like I asked you, too?"

"Hell no," I answered and continued to chew my food. I waited until I swallowed what I had in my mouth before I said anything else, because I didn't want to hear Talisha's mouth. "He's not coming to the wedding. I already told you that."

"What do you mean he's not coming to the wedding? Who do you think is doing my hair that day?"

"Shit, its other stylist in the shop that can do your hair. Ask Janea," I suggested.

"Now that's a person who will not be attending the wedding."

"Why not," I asked in Janea's defense. "That girl ain't did shit to you?" Even though she did try to give me some pussy when I first started working at Cut N' Curl. "Janea cool people."

"Ummm . . . hmmm," she uttered.

"I ain't even gon' ask what that grunt was for."

"That's because you know exactly what it was for. I don't trust that bitch no farther than I can see her."

"Okay then, if Janea can't come to the wedding then Judy can't come either." I put a chip in my mouth.

Here's the thing. I've tried to get along with Juju, but queer mothafuckas' like him really get to me. Not to mention the ego-trip he been on since he bought the shop. I would prefer if he/she not say shit to me—period! I've thought about leaving the shop all together and find somewhere else to make my dough just like Precious and Regina did when Juliana took over, but with me being the only barber in the shop, plus all of the foot traffic that comes through the shopping center; the money is too good to give it up. I tolerate all his "drag-queen antics" at work because I don't have a choice, but outside of work—fuck no; especially not on my wedding day!

Now as far as everybody else in the shop goes I'm cool with them. Angelle pretty much stays to herself, and Janea keeps me entertained with her daily updates about the niggas she fuck with— which was one of the reasons I ain't ran up in her— so other than Juju; I really don't have no complaints. I try my best to ignore his ass but he purposely does shit to annoy me, like tonight. Won't no need for him to call no damn emergency meeting, because as long as he gets his money from us every week there ain't shit for us to meet about. He acts like he signs our paychecks or something. I don't have to kiss his ass to get along with him. All I know is that he better leave me the fuck alone before I fuck him and Whitney up!

# Night and Day!

"Do you know what time it is, Rochelle?" I flung open the front door and, "Leave me alone," was the response I received.

I closed the front door, secured the locks, followed by the chain. Rochelle marched upstairs to her bedroom with my grandson straddled over her shoulder and slammed her bedroom door. I guess I should be relieved that she even came home at all. I was starting to worry about Boom-Boom and his momma, too.

Rochelle was the first to exit my premature womb, kicking and screaming, and then she quickly made way for her sister Shantelle to channel through the birth canal she paved the way for. It took several taps on Shantelle's butt before she uttered a sound, but Rochelle broadcasted to everybody in the delivery room, as if she were a cheerleader for the Dallas Cowboys, that she was here, and she's been kicking and screaming ever since. Shantelle is less combative and avoids conflict at all cost, she gets that from me, whereas, Rochelle displayed similar behavior like her father. She grew very close to Onion the last time he was released from prison before he was murdered two years ago, but Shantelle has remained right where she has been most of her life—right up under me.

I've always referred to Shantelle as my little helper, because she would often ask me when she was little if she could help out with chores around the house. She loved to assist me in the kitchen and help me with the laundry, but Rochelle was the complete opposite. I could barely get her to keep her room clean. When the twins turned thirteen, I taught Shantelle how to shampoo hair and from then on she worked in the shop with me on the weekends until she was old enough to get a job. I guess it's safe to say the twins are like night and day.

When their daddy was released from prison, and started hustling again, he would give the girls money and bought them anything they wanted, but Shantelle still came to the shop every Friday and Saturday to help me out since those were my busiest days. Rochelle preferred to hang out with her girlfriends back then, as she still does now, despite the fact that she has a child of her own.

I first hooked up with Onion when he transferred from Norview High School to the school I was attending when my family lived out Park Place. Onion lived two streets over and I would see him in the neighborhood all the time. I never said anything to him at first, especially after I found out how old he was, because I was only fifteen at the time and Onion had me by four years. And had it not been for social promotion he would've still been in the tenth grade even though he never graduated.

I got pregnant the first time Onion and I had sex and Rochelle kept the cycle going, because she too got pregnant at a young age. Onion dropped out of school after I had the twins so that I could finish on time. Actually, the girls lived with his family until I graduated from high school. We got a place together not too long after and within six months Onion was well on his way to being a career criminal.

I struggled with the girls on my own by doing hair out of our apartment, while their father went in and out of prison, until I was able to build up enough clientele to buy my first car. I went down to social services and got on the Section 8 waiting list and within a year I was approved for a two bedroom apartment out in Twin Canal, a low-income housing project in Virginia Beach. Not too long after that I started doing hair at Cut N' Curl.

We all took Onion's death really hard and even though it has been two years since he died, Rochelle is still grieving. She really loved her daddy and to her Onion could do no wrong. I disregarded all of the warning signs that Rochelle was pregnant, as far as her excessive sleeping, mood swings, weight gain, and attributed it all to stress. Shantelle was the one to inform me that her sister was with child, but Rochelle never revealed whom Boom-Boom's father was. I was the one to nick-name him Boom-Boom, and I love him with all my heart, but early motherhood is not what I wanted for either one of my girls.

The twins are the spitting image of me and for the first sixth months of their lives Onion constantly questioned me as to whom their father was because the girls have a dark skin complexion and they looked nothing like him, but what features the twins lacked as far as Onion was concerned, was made up for in our grandson. If you hold Boom-Boom's baby picture up side-by-side with a picture of Onion you'd think it was the same person and in honor of her father, Rochelle named her son Javari Rashad Harden Jr., after her daddy.

Rochelle just needed a little more time to pull herself together; we all do. I just wish the outside interference from my family and friends would stop. I'm so tired of constantly having to defend the choices I make to others outside of my household; it's none of their damn business anyway! I don't tell them how to run their lives, so I cannot understand why my life—and what goes on in it—is constantly up for a discussion.

No, I'm not going to sell my house. Onion put a sizeable down payment on it and within ten years the house will be paid for, so I would be a fool to sell it now. As far as my BMW is concerned, Onion bought the car for me around the time Milk bought Nicole's car for her, and they paid little to nothing for them because the cars were stolen, but I do have a clear title for it.

Onion hustled with Milk for years until they had a falling out behind some money, at least that's what he told me. However, Janea told me that she heard Onion beat up some girl who supposedly robbed him and that was the real reason for the altercation between him and Milk. I confronted Onion about it and he claimed there was no truth to it and for me to stop listening to that freak bitch—as he referred to Janea—and for me to never come to him with bullshit like that again.

I was tempted to knock on Rochelle's bedroom door to check on Boom-Boom, but I wasn't in the mood, nor did I have the energy to argue with his momma tonight. Instead, I'm going to climb back into my bed and pray for a better day. I'm almost afraid to see what tomorrow will bring.

"Ma, are you okay?"

"Oh, my gosh, Shantelle, you scared me." I quickly turned around. "What are you still doing up?"

"The same reason you're up. I was waiting for my sister to come home."

"She just came in. Go to bed and get you some sleep. Rochelle will be fine."

"I heard her when she came in. Ma, can I talk to you for a minute?"

"What is it Rochelle, I'm really tired?"

"Well, never mind then. It can wait," she replied.

"Are you sure?" I questioned after seeing a look of disappointment on her face.

"Yeah Ma, I'm sure. Go ahead to bed." She smiled.

"I'll see you in the morning, Shan."

"Okay. I love you." She reached out to give me a hug. I quickly backed away. I'm not really a touchy-feely kind of person.

"I love you too, baby. It's late and you have to get up early in the morning," I said with a phony smile.

"Oh, and you haven't forgotten about your appointment tomorrow have you?"

"No, I didn't forget. I'm actually looking forward to it."

# Penny and a Dime!

"Throw that pussy girl!" Terrell's voice echoed throughout the room.

"I know that's right, fuck this pussy nigga," I replied and pulled him closer to me. I see right now Terrell will be placed at the top of the *"Onion Dick"* list, 'cause his dick was so good; he damn near brought me to tears.

I don't know if the Ciroc had kryptonite mixed in with its ingredients or not, because Terrell seems to have found a source of stamina from somewhere. This is round three and he has truly giving my pussy a work-out like he was in training for the Dick Olympics, but I ain't complaining. If you ain't sore when you're finished then the nigga ain't fuck you right. Fellas, you have to fuck her like you really mean it. Get nasty if you have, too, and pull her hair while you're deep stroking her. I guarantee you she'll love it!

"Damn, you got some good pussy Janea," he moaned in between his panting.

"How good is it?" I purred.

"Girl, I could fuck you all night," he said, and then raised me up off the bed. *'Uh oh . . . some top of the dresser action. I have died and gone to Dick Heaven!'*

40

"Grip those legs back," he instructed.

"How, 'bout I just put them up here," I said, positioning my legs up on Terrell's shoulders.

"I'mma' do you one better," he replied.

Terrell now had me suspended in mid-air with my legs clamped firmly around his neck, as he propelled his "sweet meat"—that means dick— in and out of me with ease. Never one to be out done I bounced up and down on Terrell's dick like it was a Pogo stick. We made our way around the room fucking as if it was our last day on earth until we both collapse. *'Talk about calisthenics for your pussy.'*

I waited until Terrell was sound asleep before I got up out the bed to go leave. My one-hitter-quitter pussy lullabied his ass into a deep slumber, and he was now snoring like he hadn't slept in days. I never stayed out all night because I had to be home in the mornings to give Ma Pearl her medicine.

I was trying to be quiet as I tip-toed around the room gathering my clothes. I didn't want Terrell to feel as if he has to make any empty promises to me as to when we would see each other again. He can save his lies for another unsuspecting victim. Not that I wouldn't hook up with him again—his dick game was definitely on a thousand—but I'm not looking for a relationship. I came; I saw, I conquered, and now I'm on to the next one!

I will give it to Terrell though; his house is laid the fuck out. The master bedroom is somewhat smaller than most, but other than that I really like the way his place was furnished. I noticed some toys here and there when I first walked in and that told me his kids either lived here with him, or they visited him often and that's all the more reason for me to keep it moving, because I don't do baby mommas.

I was in the bathroom ready to hop in the shower to get me a quick hit-or-miss spritz before I went home when I realized I had forgotten to grab a wash cloth and a towel from the linen closet. I left the water running, opened the bathroom door, and tip-toed out in to the hallway. I peered my head into Terrell's bedroom and saw that he was still resting comfortably. I closed the linen closet door after retrieving a wash cloth and towel when I heard a clicking sound.

"Move and I'mma' blow yo' mothafuckin' brains out!" a male voiced ordered.

I was too afraid to turn around and as dark as it was in the hallway I wouldn't have been able to see who it was anyway. I started screaming loud enough to wake up Terrell up and the dead, too! Whoever it was had now turned on the lights in the hallway.

"Man, what the fuck is you doing in my got damn house, Janea? And shut up all that fucking screaming before you wake my kids up!" Milk yelled, as he lowered his gun.

"Milk, you scared the shit out of me." I breathed a sigh of relief. *'What a minute, did he just say his house?'*

"Naw, I'm sure my brother already fucked the shit out of you. Yo', Rell," he banged on Terrell's bedroom door, "man, come see yo' company out." I had forgotten for a minute that I was butt ball naked. I quickly covered myself with the towel I got out of the linen closet.

"What the fuck is you trying to cover up now for?" Milk asked with a grin on his face. "Like I ain't never seen yo' ass naked. Ain't it 'bout time for you to retire yo' warn out pussy? You should be tired of being used for nut by now."

"Fuck you mothafucka'!" I pointed in his face with my free hand. "I see your ass is still out here on the hoe stroll your damn self now that Sabrina finally got some sense and left your black ass!"

"I sure hope Rell wrapped his shit up. You know you're known for giving niggas' dick the hiccups," he shot back. "I see you keeping it all in the family. You want me to go wake my son up so you can slob him down, too?" he started laughing.

"What's up, man?" Terrell looked at his brother and then to me. "Yo', put some clothes on Shorty." He yawned.

"I see you still can't tell the difference between a penny and a dime, huh Rell?" Milk turned the hallway light off and walked away.

Fuck the shower. Let me get the hell out of here before I have to cut a motherfucka' up!

# Family Ties!

"Girl, I had my face buried in the pillow biting down on my bottom lip with my toes curled, that nigga dick was so good!"

Lawd have mercy! This bitch ought to be ashamed of her damn-self. Let her ass keep on spreading eagle for every man with a nose and a pulse and she gone end up with Carpal Tunnel of the pussy. *'Uugghh the visual.'* My stomach is churning right now just thinking about it. I used to laugh and joke with Janea about her sexual escapades and I was slightly amused by her most recent encounter she just shared with us about the light-skinned "Mandingo Warrior" she met at Harry O's last night, but now the shit is starting to become a little redundant.

I've never seen anyone so dead set against being in a relationship with one person as Janea is. And I thought gay men had a problem with monogamy. I just don't understand why she feels as if she has to reduce herself to such desperate measures. She's a very pretty girl and you know I don't pass out to many compliments with all the jealous bitches' out here, but Janea really does have a good head on her shoulders contrary to what you all may believe.

If she would just let go of some of the baggage she's carrying from past relationships and allow the right man to knock that chip off of her shoulders—instead of just knocking her off—she might just find some form of happiness. Janea doesn't even give her coochie enough time to accumulate any dust and that's not good; but who am I? I have enough of my own troubles to worry about.

After careful consideration, I've made the decision to issue Kabo a verbal written warning for in-subornation. Yes, I'm afraid it has come to this. Aaahhh . . . the pressure one is faced with when owning your own establishment. I can truly relate to Donald Trump, because it does indeed have its challenges, but I flat out refuse to put up with disgruntled employees! I've come to the conclusion that if I take down the general—Kabo— then all of his little soldiers will fall into line.

I learned that war strategy from watching *The Patriot,* starring Mel Gibson. Have you seen that movie? Good, then you know what I'm referring too. Oh, and did you see that goddess of a white boy who played the villain in that movie? What was his name . . . shit . . . it's on the tip of my tongue . . . hell, I don't know, Jason something . . . but anywho, I feel as if a verbal-written warning is in order considering the way Kabo disrupted my first meeting. Especially when I know that his constant harassment toward me only steams from the fact that I am gay.

Just because my toe-nails stay French tipped up, and I wear eyelashes to extend my naturally curly length, does not give him the right to constantly disrespect me. Yes, I do throw a few insults his way unprovoked, but it's mostly out of pure frustration. Besides, it does not compare to the God awful, outlandish things Kabo has said to me and I refuse to allow it to continue. Not in Cut N' Curl—and certainly not on my watch!

So, anyway . . . after Kabo tore the write-up into shreds right before my very eyes, I had to re-think my strategy once again. I'm going to have to come harder at this mothafucka' than I thought, and the only way I knew how to do that was to reach out to my people in the streets. I really don't like to show my dark side, but Kabo has left me no other choice. As quiet as it's kept, I'm a part of Milk's dynasty and Kabo has no idea that he's fucking with the wrong bitch! I have "family ties" to the family itself, and if he keeps fucking with me I'm just going to have Milk assassinate him.

What . . . what's so funny? Okay—maybe I did embellish just a tad bit, but Milk and I are related by marriage, and that's the tie that binds us. Well, we used to be related by marriage—but then him and Sabrina got divorced, and then got back together again; only to end the relationship once more. And chile', let me fill you in on what's going on between the two lovebirds now . . . on second thought—never you mind. I know you're tired of hearing about all that rumbling and shit. Okay, so maybe there isn't a direct bloodline between Milk and I, but Sambo doesn't know that. Milk is bringing Saysha to the shop today so I can do Little Miss Diva's hair, and we'll see how much Kabo has to say to me then—with his black ass!

# Papa Don't Take No Mess!

Now that my morning rush is over and I don't have any appointments scheduled until later on this afternoon, I decided it was a good time for me to freshen up my dread locks.

I was sitting at my station with my back to the door when I looked up and saw Milk walking into the shop carrying a little boy in his arms through the mirror. There was also a little girl with him and I figured they both were his kids. I winked at him to suggest there were no hard feelings and when he returned my gesture of good faith with a head nod I figured everything was cool between us. I've known Milk for quite a few years and had I known that Terrell was his brother I would have never gone home with him last night. I don't fuck in circles. Well, not that close together anyway.

"Juju!"

The little girl ran over to Juju's station where he was bent down waiting for her with open arms.

"Why, hello, Lil' Miss Diva." Juju scooped her up. "Look at how big you've gotten." e kissed her on the cheek. "Chile,' what has yo' father done to yo' head?" Juju looked at Milk. "Well . . . at least he tried. Let me get those sandals you have on Ms. Diva. What are they 'bout a size twelve? I think I can squeeze my feet into to them." He poked her in the stomach and put her down. "How you doing, Milk?"

"What's up?" I glanced over at Milk when I heard his irritated response to Juju's welcome.

"Welcome to the new and improved Cut N' Curl," Juju said, extending out his arms as if he were one of the chicks on *The Price Is Right*, showing off a showcase.

"Yeah, it's a'ight," Milk mumbled, as he looked around. He started laughing and shaking his head when he zoomed in on the mural of Juju and Whitney on the wall. That's usually everyone's first reaction to the buffoonery displayed for all to see.

"Hey, there mini Milk," Juju spoke to the little boy. This is the first time I've seen him since he was a year old and he favored his daddy now more than he did when he was born. He's so cute. I can't understand what would make Nicole leave her child the way she did.

"Hey there mini Milk," he repeated after Juju.

"He always copies everything people say Juju," Little Miss Diva said. "And it gets on my nerves."

"What I tell you 'bout yo' mouth, Saysha?" Milk straightened his daughter. One thing for certain, Milk sure did mark his children, because Saysha looked just like him, too. I can tell she had a lot of Sabrina in her by the way she just rolled her eyes at Milk. *'Let me turn around and mind my own business.'* "Roll 'em again, hear?" Milk dared her. I slowly twirled my chair back around just to see her reaction. *'Okay, so I'm nosey.'* Saysha hurried up and fixed her face. *'I see Papa don't take no mess!'*

"Juju, can you put some curls in my hair like how you did Whitney's hair in that picture on the wall?" Saysha pointed.

"Yes ma'am, I sure can," he answered.

Juju sat her down in his chair and then placed one of his miniature capes around Saysha's neck, and then he started looking around the shop.

"What time you want me to come pick her up?" Juju was too busy still looking around to hear Milk's question. "Yo'?"

"Oh, I'm sorry did you say something, Milk?" Juju raised his voice, and then he looked toward the backroom.

*'Who the hell is he looking for?'*

"How long you gon' be on her hair? What time do you want me to come back and pick her up?" he asked again.

"Oh, you're not gonna' wait for her?" Juju asked with a disappointed look on his face

"Naw," Milk shook his head, "I got a few things I need to take care of. Just hit me when you finished. I'll come back to get her."

Just then Kabo walked from the backroom over to his station. Juju's eyes widened and he now had a sneaky look on his face. Milk was also looking at Kabo rather strange if you ask me, and as Kabo returned Milk's gritted stare I thought for a minute there was about to be a problem.

"Okay, I will just give you a call on your personal cell phone when I'm done, Milk. I know that you're extremely busy with very important people to see. Believe me, I understand."

*'What the hell is going on? What did I miss?'*

"Whatever." Milk reached for his son's hand. "Come on Mj"

"Come on, Mj," his son repeated.

I now recognized that Mj was autistic. My Aunt Robin's son Sayvon also has autism and he used to do the same thing when he was younger. He soon grew out of it despite the fact that the doctors told my Aunt Robin that he never would.

I may have exchanged a few unpleasant remarks with Milk less than twenty-four hours ago but one thing I will give him credit for was the way that he interacted with his children. He's raising Mj by himself and it appears as if he's very active in Saysha's life as well even though she lives in Atlanta with Sabrina. *'Yeah, I still gets the inside scoop.'* Men shouldn't get any brownie points for taking care of their children, because that's what they're supposed to do, but more often than not; they don't. I respect Milk for that even though he ain't shit. He's doing right by them kids.

"I'm sorry, what did you say, Uno? Did you say something?" Kabo never answered Juju because he was still exchanging looks with Milk. "Oh, okay, I thought I heard you say something." Juju smiled. Kabo turned his back to both of them and started sanitizing his clippers.

51

*'Okay, something is up and I don't like being left out of the loop.'*

"You mind Juju, you hear me lil' girl?" Milk said with authority.

"I will. Bye Daddy, I love you. See you later Mj." Saysha waved.

"See you later Mj," he mocked his sister.

"Daddy love you, too, baby."

"Daddy, is you still gon' take us to Chucky Cheese later on?" Saysha asked with a smile on her face that would melt your heart into pieces.

"Only if you be good," Milk responded.

"I'mma' be good," she said, and blew Milk a kiss.

*'Awww . . . I wish I had a little girl sometimes.'*

# Planet Rock!

"Whewww . . . I sure could go for me a tall glass of chocolate milk!"

I saw Juju looking at me out of the corner of my eyes when he said the word "milk", and this is the bullshit I be telling Talisha about and now y'all see the shit for yourself. Twizzler is just trying to provoke me, but I'm not going to feed in to his bullshit today.

"Juju, give me some of that shit you been smoking." Janea laughed.

"Milk sure does the body good, don't it Janea?" Juju winked at me.

"Whatchu' talking about now, Juju?" Janea asked, as she applied relaxer to her client's hair.

"Angelle, do you got milk?"

Juju asked Angelle the question but he was still looking directly at me. He's trying his best to get a rise out of me for some reason, but let him keep on and I'mma' body slam his little tiny ass!

"Milk gives me gas," Angelle answered, as she walked toward the backroom. Juju's attempt to be funny went right over her head.

"Well, I guess you're right," Juju said, "Milk can also fuck a body up!" He snapped his fingers.

"What the fuck you keep looking over here at me for, Tootsie Roll? Come on man." I signaled to my client who had just walked into the shop.

"Are you referring to me, Kunta?" Juju playfully asked.

"Fuck you Rainbow Brite!" I pumped the lever on the chair to raise my client up higher and then placed a cape around his neck.

"Somebody sure has a whole lot to say all of a sudden." Juju popped his lips. "A few hours ago you were over there as quiet as a whore in church, ain't that right, Janea?" Juju sashayed toward the backroom.

*'I see right now I'm going to end up fucking this punk up today.'*

"Whatever is going on between you two, leave me out of it," Janea told him.

I don't know what the fuck Juju called himself doing when Milk was up here earlier today, but I just hope he doesn't think I'm scared of that nigga'. I'm the one who taught his ass how to get it in the streets and had I not gone to prison, along with a lot of other niggas from down the Beach back in 2000, Milk would have never been the Birdman around here. Fat mothafucka! Gritting on me and shit like I owed his ass something.

I was locked up with Milk for a little while in Mecklenburg prison but I only had six months left to do on my sentence when he got there. We had a minor disagreement about a few things but it won't nothing serious. I personally don't have a problem with Milk—shit, I ain't in the game no more anyway and the money I make is legit. We didn't knuckle up then when we were locked up together, and I'm not about to throw no blows behind no fucking Juju.

Speaking of Sweet and Sour, this mothafucka' announced to us this morning that we were no longer permitted to use his private bathroom. This homo had the audacity to tell us that for now on we had to use the same bathroom that the customers used, so I left a nice surprise in there for him and he should be twisting his ass back in here in . . . *five . . . four . . . three . . . two . . . one . . .*

"Hold the hell up!" Juju screamed. I started laughing to myself.

"Juju, what's wrong with you now?" Janea hollered out. Juju stomped from the backroom to the middle of the floor like the flaming queen she is.

"I want to know right now which one of you nasty mothafuckas' defamed my bathroom like that!" He put his hands on his hips.

"What are you talking about, Juju?" Janea asked. "How do you defame a bathroom?"

"With shit!" he hollered. "There is a turd as long as my arm floating around in my damn toilet. I specifically asked you people not to use my bathroom, didn't I?" Juju gave everyone a wide-eye look. Janea started laughing and so did some of the customers. You know I'm over here weaker than a motherfucka'!

"It won't me," Angelle said.

"It won't me either," Janea shook her head still laughing. Juju looked in my direction.

"It won't me either Boss." I sucked my teeth.

"Go 'head and laugh, Kato," he scowled. "I know it was yo' stinking ass that did that trifling shit!"

"You don't know shit, Twinkle Toes. Did you see me do it?"

"Stay yo' rusty ass out of my bathroom!" he commanded, and then twirled back over to his station. I was about to respond to Sugar Smacks, when my thoughts were interrupted by the music coming from outside.

"Rock . . . rock . . . planet . . . rock . . . don't stop . . . rock . . . rock . . . planet rock . . . don't stop . . ."

"What the fuck?" Juju looked toward the window as the base drew nearer. "Who the hell is out there blasting that old ass Planet Rock?" Everybody in the shop now had their attention focused on the window waiting to see who it was pushing the car with the booming system. I know whoever the mothafucka' is the nigga can't think while he's driving with that loud ass music playing. "Do y'all see this fuckery?" Juju shouted, and rotated his way toward the front door. I started laughing my damn self when I saw what Sweet and Low was referring, too.

'Only in Virginia.'

"Lord, I don' seen it all." Janea started laughing.

"Who in-the-fuck puts a stereo system on a fuckin' bike?" Juju hollered, as he flung the shop door open. If I wasn't here today to see this shit myself, I wouldn't believe it if somebody told me. *'What the hell is this world coming too; besides the end?'* "If you don't turn all that bumpty-bump shit off this very instance, I'mma' call the boys in blue on yo' ass!" Juju pointed at the dude with the brush he had in his hand.

"Whatchu' say?" the guy riding the bike roared over top of the music.

"Turn that shit off!" Juju screamed.

"Hold up." Dude put his hands up. "Let me turn the music off so I can hear you." Dude pressed a button on his radio silencing the music. "Ok, now whatchu' say?"

"Have you lost yo' motha-fuck-in' mind?" Juju now had his hands on his hips. "Don't you ever come to my establishment blasting all that roof is on fire shit! There are neighboring businesses in this strip mall and you have just set the black race back twenty-five years with this tomfoolery!" Juju crossed his arms around his chest. "Can I help you?"

"I got some DVD's for sale man," the man answered. He attempted to walk into the shop, but Juju quickly put his hands on the door frame, blocking his entry.

"Uhhh . . . I don't think so." Juju shook his head at the man. "I don't allow any bootlegged items to be sold in my place of business. Take yo' ass out

Park Place somewhere with yo' pirated movies. Go on." Juju swayed his hands at the man as if he was a fly.

"Come on man, these good quality DVD's. I ain't got no pirate movies, but I got some other good ones and they ain't bootlegged either," he assured Juju. "I got Starchy and Hutch. I got a two-disk set of Bonanza. You remember the Cartwrights' don't cha'? I got the complete fifth season of The Andy Griffin Show. I got the Dukes of Hazard . . ."

"That shit is as old as that Planet Rock song you were just blasting," Jolly Rancher cut him off.

"How, about The Love Boat, then?" He held up the DVD.

"I said no!" Juju stood his ground.

"Man, that's fucked up," the guy countered, shaking his head.

"No, what's fucked up is yo' old ass on that mothafuckin' bike, riding up and down the street like you Radio Raheim. Do the right thing and get the hell out of here. I ain't gon' tell yo' ass but one more time, go on now." Juju waved his hands again. "Go 'head, 'fore I call po-po on yo' ass. Get!"

"But man, I got a March Madness sale going on."

"March?" Juju wrinkled up her face. "This is mothafuckin' July, negro!"

"Okay, well I got a March Madness sale going on in July. Like Christmas in July." I looked over at

Janea and I thought she was gone pass out she was laughing so hard.

"How 'bout 'dis?" Juju raised his arm and pointed outside. "How 'bout you January, February . . . March yo' ass back up the street and take yo' Little Tikes bike with you!"

"Well, how about some can goods? Anybody in here want to buy some potted meat?" He looked over Juju's shoulder. "I got some Vienna Sausages and a couple of cans of SPAM, too."

"Don't nobody still living eat that shit!" Juju squealed. "Take them stolen can goods back to Family Dollar where you housed them from!" Juju slammed the door in his face, and pranced back over to his station like he was on a runway stage. "Let that be a lesson to all of you. I will not allow bootlegged items to be sold in my salon. Do I make myself clear, Hobo?" Juju looked directly at me.

"*One of these days,*" I thought to myself as I shook my head. "*One of these mothafuckin' days!*"

"Who was that out there making all that noise?" Angelle emerged from the backroom.

"Girl, you just missed the funniest shit," Janea told her. "What were you doing in the back for so long? I thought you had gone home."

"Rochelle has my car. She told me she was about to pull up a few minutes ago when I talked to her but when I went outside I didn't see her. Her ass is going to make me late for my appointment," she answered, as she looked down at her watch in a huff.

"You can use my car," Janea offered.

"Naw, that's alright," Angelle turned her down, "I don't know how long I'll be. I think I might just catch the bus."

"Catch the bus?" Janea frowned. "What kind of sense does that make? Call her ass back and tell her to bring you your shit."

"I know that's right," Juju added. "Does Rochelle even have driver's license?"

"Ummm . . . I would appreciate if the two of you would refrain from discussing my business in front of everyone." She rolled her eyes at them.

"Who, the fuck is she talking, too?" Juju looked at Janea.

"I'm talking to your ass Juju," Angelle hollered.

"Girl, tell me tomorrow!" Juju said. *'Tell me tomorrow is equivalent to saying, bitch boo!'* "You better go sit yo' ass down somewhere," he told her while striking a sistah' girl pose. "I refuse to entertain yo' alter ego today. Gon' somewhere and doodle in that little notebook of yours, 'cause I ain't done shit to yo' ass. Save that baritone base in yo' voice for yo' chirren'."

"Fuck you Juju!"

Honey Nut Cheerios' eyes widened at Angelle's comeback. *'I know that's right Angelle; cuss that bitch out!'*

"Oh, no my darling, you could never fuck this," Juju snapped back. "I don't do fish!"

*'You know I'm over here cracking the fuck up. I love to see two women go at it.'* "But I'mma' tell

you what you can do . . ." Juju shimmed over toward Angelle. "You can get the fuck out my shop!"

# One Out Of Two!

I grabbed my purse off my station, stormed out of the salon, and slammed the door behind me. I prayed to God that the glass would shatter—but no such luck. I'm tired of Juju's shit and you best believe I gave his ass a piece of my mind before exiting Cut N' Curl. There are too many shops in the area that I could work at, so I don't have to put up with his foolishness! I have been doing hair at Cut N' Curl for almost ten years and to be perfectly honest; the salon should be mine. I started off in the salon shampooing hair for Lea—the former owner—and I would've bought the shop from her myself if I had the money at the time.

Rochelle still hadn't come to pick me up and she's not answering her cell phone either. I should've never let her use my car in the first place. I haven't caught the bus in damn near ten years and I have no clue as to when the next bus is going to come. I saw a few people gathered at the bus stop so it must be coming soon.

"Sir, do you know what time the next bus comes?" I asked an older gentleman who was waiting at the bus stop.

"It will be along sooner than later," he answered.

"How much does it cost to ride the bus?"

"Depends on where you going. The bus that's coming along in a few minutes is going to the TCC Campus in Virginia Beach, and if you're not getting off there you have to pay another fare," he explained.

"Well, that's almost close to where I'm going. How much is the fare?" I felt around in my purse for my wallet.

"Just get an all-day pass," a woman standing next to me answered for him.

"Thank you." I smiled at her. The bus had just pulled up and I still hadn't found my wallet.

"You getting on," the bus driver asked me.

"I'm sorry." I walked up the two steps to get on the bus. "I need an all-day pass." I looked inside of my purse again. *'Where the hell is my wallet?'*

"I'm going to be late for work," one of the passengers on the bus hollered out.

"Here," the older man said, extending his hand out to me. "You can have these two dollars. This will take you to the next stop."

"Sir, you don't have to do that," I said, turning down his money.

"Miss, I got a schedule to keep," the bus driver warned.

The older gentleman who offered to pay my fare reached around me and slid the money into the slot and then he told me to go sit down. I reluctantly accepted his kind gesture and moved out of the way to allow the other passengers to board the bus. I strolled toward the back of the bus and sat down in the first empty seat I came to. I then started fishing through my purse again for my wallet. After taking everything out and placing its contents on the empty seat next to me, I concluded that my wallet just wasn't there.

"That damn Rochelle," I said aloud to myself.

She must've stolen it again. *Shit!* Now I don't have any money to pay for another fare. I took a deep breath and looked around to see if there was anyone on the bus that I knew. After a quick scan of the passengers behind me, I mentally started to prepare myself for the thirty-minute walk to my doctor's appointment. I swear if it weren't for buzzard luck I wouldn't have any luck at all.

I sat back in my seat to enjoy what little comfort I did have for the time being and took notice of all the different people riding the bus. There was a white man dressed in a pinstriped suit and he looked so out of place amongst the many black people that filled seats. My immediate thoughts were, "Didn't he have a car? Surely he did, so what was he taking the bus for?"

Sitting behind me were two young girls who could not have been any more than sixteen—if that—and they were having themselves a good old time laughing amongst each other.

"Girl, I told him that he was going to have to buy me a new pair off tennis shoes if he was gon' hit this," one of the girls said.

"I know that's right, girl," her friend agreed.

"Shoot, my momma ain't raise no fool. I did give him some head behind the bleachers after he finished football practice though," she added. "He hasn't called me since then but I know he's just busy with football practice and er'thing."

"Don't worry 'bout that girl he definitely gon' call you. Did you suck his dick like we practice at my house on the banana?" her friend asked.

I know that I'm not the only one on the bus who could hear their conversation as loud as they were talking. It made me think back to when I was their age and I wondered if I was as naive as these two young ladies seemed to be. I kind of felt sorry for them. It was obvious that they're both beyond clueless. I wanted to turn around so bad and tell them two honeys that they should be concentrating more on getting their education versus worrying about some little boy who probably can't even pee straight yet. I wish someone had of pulled me aside when I was their age and schooled me, but then again, what really did I teach Rochelle?

*"Next stop . . . TCC at the Virginia Beach campus . . ."* a recording chimed, indicating the stop was coming up.

Damn, I really don't feel like walking. I reached inside of my purse for my cell phone to call Rochelle again.

"Answer the phone," I said to myself.

"Hello?"

"Rochelle, where are you?"

"I'm doing something right now!" she answered with an attitude.

"You're doing something?" I responded with just as much attitude. "Didn't I tell you that I had an appointment this afternoon when you dropped me of at work this morning?" She didn't respond. "Hello?"

"I'll call you back, I'm busy."

"Rochelle?" I called out her name. "Rochelle?" I raised my voice.

"Miss, you gon' have to keep it down," the bus driver advised me. I looked up at him through his rear-view mirror.

"Sorry," I said as I rolled my eyes up at the ceiling of the bus.

I looked down at my cell phone and saw that my call with Rochelle was still connected. I called out her name again and she didn't answer, but I did hear something that really caught my attention. I pressed the phone to my ear, and placed my other hand on the opposite ear to drown out the chatter from the people on the bus. I heard voices and I was for certain one of them belonged to my daughter, but I couldn't make out what they were saying.

"Rochelle?" I called her name again.

I then heard what sounded like moaning. I took the phone away from my ear to check the volume to make sure it was turned all the way, and then put the phone back up to my ear.

*'I know damn well her ass is not having sex right now while my ass on the fucking bus!'*

Yep—it was definitely moaning.

"Rochelle!" I screamed into the phone again. Everyone on the bus was looking at me now.

"Miss, you gon' to have to pay another fare or get off at this stop," the bus driver said in an agitated tone. "I told you before I have a schedule to keep."

I looked at my cell phone again and it displayed a picture of my grandson. Rochelle must've realized that she had not hung up the phone and disconnected the call. I threw my phone inside of my purse and stood up to get off the bus. I was about to walk down the steps when a man that had just gotten off of the bus turned around and asked me if I needed a day-pass.

*"Oh, I could kiss you right now,"* were my immediate thoughts. "Thank you so much." I started to tell him that my feet thanked him, too.

"No problem. I don't need it anymore today." He smiled.

I waited until the rest of the passengers exited the bus before I got back on. I swiped the day-pass, and then returned to the seat I was sitting in. I tried calling Rochelle again but she must've turned her cell phone off, because it went straight to voicemail after the first ring. I wonder where Boom-Boom is since his momma was busy getting her freak on. I need to just take custody of him, because Rochelle has proven to me repeatedly that she is unfit to take care of him.

Once I finally reached my destination, I raced off the bus toward the Pembroke One building trying my best to make it to my appointment on time. I wasn't for sure what floor the office was on and after a quick scan of the directory I got on the elevator headed up to the third floor.

"Hi, my name is Angelle Turner. I have an appointment with Shareese Vawters."

"You can go ahead and have a seat," the receptionist advised after sliding the glass window to the right. "I'll page her and let her know that you are here." She smiled.

"Thank you."

I sat down in a chair in the corner, and then I flipped through the pages of my notebook until I came to a clean sheet of paper. I grabbed a pen out of my purse and started writing.

*Today I feel like fighting—and I know you want to know, why.*

*I'm tired of putting on a happy face—just to get by . . .*

"Angelle?"

"I'm right here." I raised my hand. I closed up my notebook and put my purse on my shoulders.

"You can come on back." She smiled. I stood up, took a deep breath and followed her down the hall to a corner office. "Have a seat," she said, and closed the door once we were inside her office.

Dr. Vawters sat down in the single chair and I sat on the chase directly across from her. You would have thought it was dark outside because the room was so dimly lit. I noticed a framed picture on Dr. Vawters' desk. I assume the people in the picture with her were her family. They all looked so happy. You could see it in their eyes and I became instantly jealous of Dr. Vawters even though I've only known her for two minutes. Before I knew it; I was crying. I couldn't tell you what I was crying for at this very moment, because I really didn't know myself. Through my fogged haze of tears, I saw Dr. Vawters reach over and pick up a box of Kleenex off of the end table next to her.

"Thank you," I said, as she passed me a single tissue.

"It's alright Angelle. Take as much time as you need," Dr. Vawters said in a comforting manner.

Apart of me was starting to regret even coming to see her today, but I am at my wits end and if something in my life doesn't changed—and I mean soon—I am going to officially lose what little bit of sanity I have left.

"I'm sorry." I shook my head.

"It's okay. Just take a few deep breathes Angelle, and we can begin whenever you're ready." I let go of a long sigh, wiped my face with the damp tissue, and then I told Dr. Vawters that I was ready to begin. "What brings you here to see me today?"

I pondered over her question before I responded. My momma raised us with the understanding that you should never tell your business to anyone; especially not a perfect stranger. One of her favorite quotes was, "What goes on in my house, stays in my house," and I have lived by that code pretty much all of my life. Well, at least I tried to anyway. Janea has really been the only person I would confide in, but I also knew that she likes to runs her mouth, too.

"I don't even know where to start. Can I have another tissue to blow my nose?"

"Absolutely." She reached for another tissue. "Here, just take the box and sit it down next to you on the table." I pulled out two more tissues and then placed the box down on the table. "Angelle, this is the one place where you don't have to be afraid. Anything that is said between these four walls is just between us."

"I hate my life," I quickly admitted.

"What exactly does that mean you hate your life? You hate some of the choices that you've made, or is it that you hate the direction you see your life going in?" she asked for clarity.

"Both." I blew my nose.

"How long have you felt this way?"

"For years," I answered immediately.

"Well, let's start with that. We're going to travel back in time if you will, and what I mean by that is, I want you to think about the first time you ever felt overwhelmed with sadness. Take a minute and think about it before you answer."

"I really don't have to think about it . . . what should I call you?"

"Shareese is fine. I'm very informal when it comes to certain things and my name is one of them. I try to make my patients feel as comfortable as possible."

"I got pregnant with my twins when I was only fifteen and I gave birth to them on their father's birthday. My pregnancy was very high risk because of my age of course and I was forced onto bed rest when I was seven months."

"How did you feel about being pregnant at such a young age?"

"To be honest, I really didn't know how to feel. I ignored the changes in my body when I started to feel them because I still wanted to go outside with my friends and do all of the things I used to do.

"Like what?"

"Like, going to house parties, after school games, sleepovers and stuff like that, but once I started to show my momma locked me down in the house like I was in prison."

"And how did that make you feel?"

"It made me feel like she was ashamed of me. My momma has always been very active in church and when she found out I was pregnant the first thing that came out of her mouth was, 'What are my church members going to say?' like I really cared." I folded my arms across my chest.

"Is that when the feelings of sadness came upon you?"

"No, not really," I replied. "It wasn't until my doctor put me on bed rest. I was so uncomfortable carrying the twins. I always felt like I couldn't get enough air to breathe and I couldn't sleep either. I was just plain old miserable," I reminisced.

"Well, that's not uncommon for any woman to feel during pregnancy. So, you've told me how you felt physically, how did it make you feel emotionally?"

"What do you mean?"

"Were you able to bond with your children as you carried them while you were feeling so much discomfort?"

"I don't understand what it is you're asking me."

"I guess what I'm trying to ask you Angelle, is if you were looking forward to motherhood at all?"

"To tell the truth," I shook my head, "no. I was still a child myself. I wasn't ready to be anybody's mother."

"Do you remember when you made the choice to have sex for the first time," she asked.

"I didn't make the choice," I snapped. "Their daddy made it for me."

"How so?" she probed.

"He told me if I loved him I would do it. Onion said that everybody else in school was doing it. Of course I know better now, but back then I didn't have a clue as to what we were doing. My momma never talked to me about stuff like that."

"Why did you agree to do it?"

"I don't know." I hunched my shoulders. "I thought that he would find somebody else to be his girlfriend if I didn't do it."

"How were you able to move past the sadness you felt back then?"

"I didn't. I've never gotten over the sadness. I've always found ways to block everything out of my mind."

"Such, as?"

"Shareese, is that all you're going to do is ask me question after question?"

"How else are we going to get to the root cause of what's troubling you, Angelle, if I don't ask you questions?" I rolled my eyes to the ceiling and exhaled another deep sigh.

"There goes another question. Can't you just give me something to make me feel better?"

"What, such as an anti-depressant?"

"Right about now I don't care what it is. I just need something to relax my mind so I can focus for five minutes."

"Angelle, I don't prescribe anti-depressants or any other kind of drugs to my patients. I prefer to take a more holistic approach toward treating depression and anxiety through physiotherapy and meditation."

"Well, I'm in the wrong place then." I stood up and put my purse on my shoulder. "My daughter was the one who suggested that I come see you in the first place. This was just a waste of my time."

"I know Shantelle very well," she mentioned. "I am the youth coordinator at the church Shantelle and I both attend. One thing I will tell you is that you've raised a very smart young lady and you should be very proud of yourself."

"I take it you've never meet my other daughter Rochelle."

"No, I haven't."

"Well, I guess one out of two ain't bad." I opened the door to leave.

"Angelle?" I turned around. "I'm here for you whenever you need me. All you have to do is call and make an appointment. I hope to see you again."

"I doubt it." I closed the door behind me. All I want to do now is go home and climb in the middle of my bed. I am sick of people for one day.

# Here Comes the Bullshit!

Angelle must've thought twice about the show she put on for everybody at the shop earlier today, because when I went out to my truck after work I found a note under the windshield wiper—addressed to yours truly—from her. I love Angelle like a feign loves crack—R.I.P. Yvette—but she has just got to snap out of this funk she has been in for the last two years. I simply won't tolerate it any longer, especially when it's taking away from her job performance. You should see some of the hairstyles she's done lately. One of her clients left the shop one day looking like Shenene from the TV show *Martin*, after she got up out of Angelle's chair. I'm going to let it slide this time, but one more blatant display of in-subordination, as well as disrespect, and she will be following Kabo's big-head ass straight down to Virginia Beach Boulevard to the unemployment office.

I decided to stop by my parent's house to pay my mother a visit since my Bear, Mike, is working late tonight. No, I don't mean "bear" as in an animal. A Bear is what we call a heavy-set man in the gay community. What . . . you've never heard of a Bear before? Chile' that's just one of the many different jargons used in the community and believe it or not there is a certain criteria you have to meet in order to be considered a Bear —or you will be shunned! That's right . . . can you believe that shit? There's actually discrimination amongst folks who are already being discriminated against by society; but you go figure.

Every year there's a big convention in Chicago that Mike and I attend strictly for Bears, so you can imagine how I'm treated being that I'm only 5'7, with a body that won't quit. Those jealous bitches can't stand my ass. I usually get the cold shoulder until they find out I'm there with Mike. Older gay men are referred to as Wolves, but they looked more like Silverbacks if you ask me. It's no different than gay men referring to each other as the Kids. I think Janet Jackson started that revolution. I don't know who categorized all of this other shit. Lions, Tigers, and Bears—oh my!

"Hello, Madre," I greeted my mother and closed the front door behind me.

"Hey, Julius, how's my handsome son doing?" she asked, as she climbed down from the ladder.

"I'm doing well." I pulled her toward me to give her a hug.

"Where's that pretty little dog of yours?

"She's over at her cousin Saysha's house visiting for a little while. I'm going to swing by there and pick her up on my way home. And what have I told you about climbing up on that ladder by yourself?"

"Somebody has to clean the dust off these filthy blades. You know your lazy tail father ain't gon' do it. Turn around and let me look at you, son." I did a quick spin. "Look at you looking all business like," she said in a proud mother's voice. "I'm so proud of you Julius."

"Thank you Mother," I replied, as I kissed her on the cheek. "You want me to finish wiping down the blades for you?" I sat my briefcase down on the dining room table.

"I'm all done now."

"Okay, I'll just put this heavy ladder away for you," I volunteered.

"I got it!" a raspy voice charged. It was my father.

"How are you doing, Father?" I quickly grabbed my briefcase from of the dining room table.

"Umph . . ." he muttered, as he folded up the ladder. "What's for dinner, Julia?" he asked my mother.

"Your plate is in the microwave," my mother informed him. "Julius, I just love that briefcase. Look at your son, Rufus." She tapped my father on his arm. "Doesn't he look handsome?"

"What did you say you cooked," he asked, ignoring mother's praises of me. I flopped down on the couch, crossed my legs, and released a useless sigh.

"What's the matter, Julius?" mother asked.

"I had to fire an employee today," I revealed. *'Well, technically I didn't fire Angelle, but I was about to, so shut up!'* I looked at my father to see if he was paying attention to what I was saying and as usual; he wasn't "I tell you, Mother, ever since I took over the establishment, I've had one challenge after the other." I shook my head. "Dad, have you ever had to fire anyone before?"

"Nope," he quickly answered. "All of my employees have respect for me."

*'Was that an insult? Okay, here comes the bullshit!'*

"Well, I'm sure my employees respect me as well, Dad. I just think the change in ownership may be the problem at hand."

"You just do what you have to do Julius," mother said. "I'm going to warm your plate up Rufus."

"So, Dad," I sat up in the chair, "when are you going to come down and check out my shop?" My mother stopped and turned around. I guess she was waiting to hear my father's response, too.

"I'm busy. I don't have time." Mother's face read one of disappointment by my father's reply and I can imagine what mines looked like. She continued onward to the kitchen and never said a word.

"I have the shop open on Sunday's now, too, so maybe you could come by then," I told my father.

"Sunday is my day of rest. Un-like you, I practice the teachings of the Bible. Instead of fooling around with women's hair all day maybe you should make a guest appearance in church sometimes," he pointed at me.

I felt like I was sixteen again and I could see a look of disenchantment on his face right now, and it was the same as the one he had when I told my parents that I was gay. I looked over at the front door when the alarm forewarned that it had been opened.

"What's going on, Pops?" It was my younger brother Jarrett.

"Hey, son." My father smiled for the first time since I've been here.

'*Welp, time to go!*'

Jarrett leaned the fishing rod he was totting in his hand up against the wall, and then sat his tackle box down on the floor next to it. I assumed that he and my father were about to go fishing.

"What's going on, Juju?" my brother asked.

"Hey," I responded dryly with a twist of my wrist.

"Pops and I are heading out to Lynnhaven Pier in a little while, why don't you come with us?" he offered.

"No thank you," I respectfully declined his invitation. I stood up with my briefcase in hand so I could leave before my mother came back from the kitchen and forced me to go fishing with them as she has done many times before. "I have a few business mechanisms to review tonight for a very important meeting I have tomorrow morning," I lied.

"I've been meaning to come by Cut N' Curl to check you out. Congratulations big brother." Jarrett raised his hand as if he wanted me to dap him up. *'Sorry, Juju don't do that.'*

"Now how you gon' find time to do that, Jarrett, between your job at the bank, Belinda and the kids, coaching little Jarrett's football and basketball team? It's a wonder you have time to sleep. I don't see how you do it."

*'I can read in between the lines.'*

"Jarrett, let me translate what Father just said," I told my little brother.

"Julius," my mother called my name.

"Oh, good, Mother you're just in time. You see Jarrett, in other words what he is sublimely saying to you is not waste your time visiting my little ole' Juke Joint. You're the good son with the wife, two and a half kids, dog, cat, and white picket fence."

"Come on now, Juju, I don't think that's what Pop meant at all," Jarrett defended him.

"That's right baby," my mother co-signed Jarrett's statement. "Why don't you go fishing with your daddy and your brother, Julius?"

"Stop babying him Julia. That's his problem now, you always fussing over him," my father said.

"Rufus go on in the kitchen and eat your food before it gets cold," mother urged. I know she was only trying to defuse the situation before it got ugly, but it was a little too late for that at this point.

"Good day, Mother!"

And with that; I left.

I don't care what I do it's never been good enough for my father. I could be the President of the United States of America, and he would still find a way to bash it. I understand that he is not in agreement with my lifestyle choice, but Jarrett is not his only son. What about me?

* * *

"Juju?" I heard the front door close and footsteps trampling up the stairs. "Where are you, babe?"

I dabbed my face with a Kleenex, and sat up in chair. *'Get it together bitch!'* I told myself.

"I'm in your office," I answered.

"Why are you sitting in here in the dark," Mike asked, flicking the light switch on. "What's wrong?"

"Nothing," I turned my head the other way. I didn't want Mike to see how upset I was.

"So, you're sitting in the dark crying for no reason?"

"I'm not crying." I flashed him a phony smile. Mike sat down in the chair across from me and loosened his tie.

"The only time you get this upset is when you have been around your father. What happened, Juju?"

"He's just a mean old bastard. What else is new?"

"Juju, you have to let that shit with your dad go. I told you that a long time ago babe."

"I don't want to talk about it right now." I got up out of the chair and walked out of Mike's office leaving him alone.

"You may not want to talk about it, but I do. You don't have anything to prove to him, Juju." Mike followed me into the bedroom.

"What is that supposed to mean?" I snarled. "I'm not trying to prove shit to him."

"Baby, don't take this the wrong way, but I want the old Juju back." Mike sat down on the bed and kicked off his shoes.

"You want the old Juju back?" I threw my hands up in air and yelled. "I ain't gon' no damn where!"

"That's not what I mean, Juju, and you know it. Ever since you bought Cut N' Curl, you've changed into a different person. You-"

"I've changed how?" I interrupted him.

"You know what . . . I'll talk to you after you have calmed down."

"No Mike, speak yo' mind. Say what the fuck you got to say!" I stared at him while batting my eyelashes.

"You need to calm your ass down!" Mike yelled back, and stood up. "You may not see it, but I damn sure do. You can own twenty Cut N' Curls', and it still won't change the relationship you have with your father, Juju." Whitney ran into our bedroom and started barking. "I'm going to take a shower." He left out of the bedroom and walked across the hall

I must say, I'm a little stunned. Mike has never talked to me that way before—even though I cuss his ass out on the regular. Don't worry; he likes it. Men love it when you talk shit to them—but do not try this at home. You're liable to end up with tinted eyes and swollen lips listening to me.

*'Oh my Lord . . . have I been that bad? Or even worse . . . have I turned into a jealous bitch?'*

"Has your momma been acting up, Whitney?" I lifted her up into my arms.

*"Roof . . . roof . . . roof . . ."*

Oh, my goodness . . . my baby just cussed me out in dog language. I guess if I ever needed a voice of reason, Mike surely was that voice. I'm still gone check his ass when he gets out of the shower for cussing at me—I'm the only hell raiser around here—but I'm going to do it in a subtle way. I love Mike, only because he loves me; flaws and all.

"Okay, Whitney, it's time for you to go to bed. Mommy and Daddy have some making up to do." I put her down in her bedroom and closed the door.

As for the rest of y'all jealous bitches, I don't do no damn peep shows. Smooches!

# Fresh to Def!

"Hey, Shantelle," I walked inside of the house. "Where your momma at?"

"Hi, Ms. Janea." She smiled. "She's upstairs in her room."

"Girl, don't call me that," I laughed. "Janea is cool with me. I thought she won't home for a minute 'cause I didn't see her car outside."

"Rochelle hasn't come back with it yet," she said, closing the door behind me. "Can I get you anything?"

"No, baby, I'm good. Whatchu' doing in the house on a Friday night?"

"I have to work early in the morning and plus I had Bible study at the church tonight."

"I know that's right. Praise the Lord. Pray for your Auntie Janea the next time you go, hear?" Shantelle started laughing.

"I will, but are you sure you don't want anything to eat or drink? I just made some Chicken Alfredo?"

"No thank you. I try not to eat too many carbs, but thanks anyway." I went up the stairs. I know Angelle wishes she had swallowed the half of Onion's nut that fertilized the egg that produced Rochelle. Shantelle is nothing like her sister, and I can't stand that strumpet. "Bitch is you decent?" I banged on Angelle's bedroom door.

"Come in, Janea." I turned the doorknob, and then walked into her room.

"You said that like I'm bothering you or something. And why the hell aren't you answering your damn phone, heifer?" I closed the door behind me.

"Isn't that what people do when they don't feel like talking?" she answered in a sarcastic tone.

I decided it was going to be up to me to be the peacemaker and bring some order to the shop. Shit has gotten way out of control and I can't work under those conditions. I set the peace treaty in motion earlier today when I put a note on Juju's truck like it was from Angelle, with the hopes that he would allow her to come back to the shop. Angelle can act like she's Proud Mary if she wants to; but it's rough out here. Now it's time for me to plead Juju's case on his behalf.

"What are you writing," I asked with my neck outstretched.

"Nothing," she said, and then closed the notebook.

"Every time I turn around you got your head buried in that notebook. Let me see it." I reached for it.

"No, Janea!" She raised the notebook up in the air. "It's none of your business. What are you doing here anyway?"

Rayven Skyy

"What was that all about today?" I sat down at the foot of the bed.

"You should be asking Juju that," she snapped, and placed the notebook on the nightstand next the bed.

"I did. Juju tried calling you," I said, beginning my series of lies, "but you didn't answer the phone. Juju said that he was sorry Angelle, and he wants you to come back to work tomorrow."

"Fuck Juju!" she yelled. "I'm sick of his bullshit." I looked at Angelle in astonishment. I know Juju pissed her off, but I've never seen her so upset as she has been lately.

"Angelle, what's really going on with you?"

"There's nothing going on with me. I'm just tired of being everybody's door mat to wipe their fucking feet on. He didn't have to carry on the way he did today."

"And neither did you," I challenged. "Angelle, you can talk to me, you know that don't you?"

"Janea, I don't feel like talking because there's nothing to talk about. I'm not going back. I told you the other night that I was going to find me another salon to work in. You can have Juju's ass. I'm done."

"Angelle, look how long we've worked at Cut N' Curl and put up with Lea's shady ass. I know Juju can be a bit much at times, but you don't ever let nobody stop you from making your money," I said in a calming voice.

86

"Janea, you might as well save your breath. I'm not going back," she refuted.

*'I see this ain't gon' be as easy as I thought.'*

"Ma-Ma, open dis' doe'," a tiny voice said from the other side of the door. It was Boom-Boom.

"Ma-Ma coming," Angelle answered her grandson, and got up from off of the bed.

"We're not finished talking about this Angelle," I told her. She opened the door to let her grandson in.

"There go Ma-Ma's little man," she said as she scooped Boom-Boom up in her arms, "Ma-Ma missed her baby. Gimme' kiss." He curled up his tiny lips to give Angelle what she requested. Boom-Boom was just as happy to see his grandmother as she was to see him. I took notice of the clothes he had on and they were filthy. Rochelle don't make no damn sense. I can't stand bitches like her that keep themselves "fresh to def" and dress the kids any kind of way. "Did you eat?" Angelle asked him.

"No." Boom -Boom shook his head.

"Come on Janea, so I can fix him a plate. Come on Javari. Your Aunt Shantelle cooked dinner tonight," she told him. "You want some noodles and chicken?"

"No," he cried. I got up and followed Angelle down the stairs to the kitchen. "Ma-Ma, I want some hotdogs," Boom-Boom specified, as Angelle strapped him into his high chair. I sat down at the kitchen table across from him.

"Ma-Ma gon' fix you some real food. I told your momma to stop feeding you that crap," she mumbled.

"His momma is right here," Rochelle said, emerging from the adjoining family room.

"Where have you been, Rochelle? And give me my damn car keys!" Angelle held her hand out.

"Your damn car keys are on the counter if you would look," she bucked back, and then opened the refrigerator door.

'*Shut up Janea,*' I told myself.

"And you don't tell me what to feed him. That's my son, not yours," Rochelle raised her voice.

'*Punch her in her fucking mouth Angelle!*' I was about to get up and leave, but something told me I'd better stay.

"Who do you think you're talking to like that, Rochelle?" Angelle questioned with a raised eyebrow.

"You," she answered her momma's question with a little sass.

'*Umph . . . Umph . . . Umph . . . It couldn't be me. I would have pulled that bitch's tonsils out by now!*'

"Rochelle, please stop," Shantelle pleaded.

"Go somewhere and pray Shantelle. Won't nobody talking to your ass anyway," Rochelle replied to her twin sister.

"You are so ungrateful. Ma didn't have to let you use her car and then you stay gone with it all day." Shantelle shook her head.

Looking at the twins stand side-by-side, you wouldn't even know that they were related to one another. Rochelle wore a Mohawk with the sides of her hair completely shaved, and she had more tattoos and piercings on her body than Dennis Rodman. She needs to start spending her money at Baby Gap for Boom-Boom instead of herself, because the skirt she has on was two sizes too small.

Shantelle has a more reserved look than her sister. She kept the long tresses Angelle took such good care of over the years and it flowed down her back effortlessly. Rochelle had the same long tresses as her twin until she took it upon herself to do a Brittney Spears, and cut it all off. I told Angelle she only did it to spite her. One thing I will say for the duo is that they both could be models, especially with their smooth, blemish free chocolate skin. And they're both just as tall as I am.

"Tell her ass again, Shantelle!" *'Shit, I couldn't hold my tongue any longer.'* I saw the look of disgust Rochelle had on her face regarding my comment, and before she had a chance to say some stupid shit out of her mouth I told her, "Mind your words lil' girl." I stood up. "I ain't your momma."

"You're right . . ." she hesitated. I'm sure it was because of the *"say some smart shit if you want to"* look I had on my face right now, but then she continued on with her statement anyway.

"Therefore, this discussion has nothing to do with you."

"Angelle, you better get her," I said and directed my attention toward Boom-Boom. "You ready to eat-eat?"

"Don't say shit to my child," Rochelle said, and then slammed the refrigerator door shut.

"Rochelle!" Angelle took a step closer to her daughter.

"Angelle!" Rochelle returned her mother's frustration. "You need to check your friend," she glanced at me before walking out of the kitchen. It was taking everything in me right now to keep from beating the brakes off her ass. I know she's a minor, but I would gladly take a charge for this chick!

"Janea, I'm sorry." I could tell Angelle was embarrassed.

"Ain't no need for you to apologize to me. You should be too busy pulling your foot out of her ass to do that. Angelle, I don't see how you put up with it."

"Me either, Ms. Janea," Shantelle concurred. Angelle didn't respond to either one of us.

After another thirty minutes of trying to convince Angelle to come back to work—to no avail—I left. I was about to get inside of my car when I noticed a dent the size of a soccer ball on the passenger side of Angelle's BMW. I started to call Angelle's cell phone to tell her to come outside, but I quickly changed my mind, because if Rochelle says anything else to me out the way tonight I am going to cave her chest in. That's Angelle's problem to deal with. If she likes it; I love it. Besides, I got some Nu-Nu waiting on me.

# Til' Death Do Us Part!

"Owww . . . baby, not too hard."

"Just relax Talisha, it's almost in," I told her and spread her butt cheeks further apart.

"Owww . . . no Kabo, I don't want to do this anymore." She said as she turned over and laid flat on her back.

"You always give up too soon. I'm telling you Boo once I get the head in it won't hurt as much," I reassured her.

"That's what you always say. No Kabo, I'm just not into that," Talisha shook her head.

"I guess I can add that to the list of shit you not into, huh?" I sat up on the side of the bed.

"And what is that supposed to mean," Talisha asked, now raised up on her elbows.

"Just what I said," I turned around to face her. "Kabo I don't want to do this! Kabo, I'm not into that! And y'all women wonder why niggas cheat."

"So what the fuck are you trying to say? You gon' go out there and start fucking around on me because I won't let you fuck me in my ass?" she raised her voice.

"Talisha, I don' told yo' ass about yelling at me like I'm a fucking child or something. You might as well get that shit out of yo' system before we walk down this aisle and jump the broom, or-"

"Or else what?" she cut me off.

"See there, I won't even gon' say or else what. I was getting ready to say after we're married I have license to whip yo' ass when you step out line." Talisha and I starred at each other for a split second before we both started laughing.

"I wish the fuck you would put your damn hands on me." I pulled the covers back and laid down next to Talisha. "What the fuck is it with y'all niggas nowadays when it comes to the ass? Me and some of the girls at work where just talking about this shit the other day. Y'all so quick to want to have anal sex with us but as soon a finger gets within a centimeter of y'all's asshole then it's, 'Hell nawl, don't fuck with my ass!' I don't understand it."

"Bring yo' ass over here," I said, pulling her closer to me. "A'ight, I get it. Damn. As long as you don't start telling me no when it comes to this pussy," I patted Talisha in between her legs. "Then that's good enough for me."

"Ummm . . . do that again," she hummed.

"What this?" I patted the kitty a second time.

"Yes baby, that feels so good," she said, spreading her legs further apart.

I climbed over top Talisha, position myself in between her legs, and now I had my tongue all down her throat. Our bodies meshed together as one and Talisha wrapped her legs around my waist.

I reached down to feel the moisture that was leaking on my thighs and as hard as my dick was I didn't have to guide it into the warm hole that awaited me, so I plunged right in.

"I'm gonna' be fucking this pussy for the rest of my life," I whispered in Talisha's ear. "I love you, baby." I thrust myself deeper inside.

"Til' death do us part," she moaned.

"You better know it!"

I put the loving on Talisha, as only I could do, up until it was time for her to go to work. It was her week to pull the overnight shift at the hospital, so I decided to hang out with the fellas for a little while tonight since tomorrow was my day off.

"Yo'?" I answered my phone.

"I'm outside nigga. Bring yo' slow ass on before I leave you. You ain't here me out here blowing the horn?" Ghost shouted through the phone.

"Naw man, I just hopped out the shower. Give me five minutes," I told him and hung up my cell phone.

I already had my clothes laid out on the bed, so it only took me a few minutes to get dressed.

"My fault," I told Ghost when I got inside of the car.

"Man, you fucking up the game. I should have left yo' ass," he said before pulling off.

"Nigga, I could have driven my own shit. You the one insisted on coming to pick me up. Where the hell is we going anyway?"

"To yo' first bachelor party."

"What? Whatchu' mean the first bachelor party?"

"You heard me nigga. Just sit yo' soon to be married ass back. Yo' best man got this." Ghost nodded his head."

"Man, what the fuck is you up to?" I started laughing.

"Look, I'mma' see to it that you get as much pussy as you can before the big day. Then maybe you will change yo' mind about getting married in the first place."

"There you go with that bullshit again," I said as I reclined the seat back. "I love my woman and right around this time next month I'mma' give her my last name. I do my shit here and there but it ain't nothing like coming home to a good woman."

"Man, save all of that Tyler Perry bullshit!" Ghost gawked at me and waved his hand. I started laughing again.

"That's why Talisha can't stand yo' ass now," I told him.

"I don't give a fuck. That's yo' headache to deal with but you can hook me up with her sister Stesha though," he threw in.

"Shit, you ain't nowhere when it comes to Stesha. Talisha will cuss you the fuck out but Stesha will cut you the fuck up!"

"I see Talisha still going through yo' cell phone."

"Whatchu' talking 'bout?" I looked at him.

"She sent me a text message the other day like she was you." Ghost was the one laughing now.

*'I see right now Imma' have to start locking my shit.'*

"No she didn't, did she? How you know it won't me?"

"How many times have you ever sent me a text message, Kabo?"

"Shit, never," I told him.

"Exactly," he smirked. "Real niggas don't send text messages to each other. That shit is unnatural if you ask me," Ghost said. "But when she texted me and asked when was she going to see me again, I knew it was her ass for sure then."

"Were the fuck is we going, Ghost?" I asked when I saw that we were about to go through the Portsmouth tunnel.

"Tone and Rick gon' meet up with us at Forbidden City," he answered.

"Ain't that Milk spot?"

"Yeah, and I'm a VIP in that mothafucka' now," he gloated.

"Man, I don't really fuck with that nigga to tough and I really ain't trying to roll up there tonight."

"Yousa' mothafuckin' lie. Nigga I already don' spent money to get the VIP room."

"And who the fuck asked you, too?" I raised my voice. Had I known this shit I would have stayed my ass home but once we pulled up in the parking lot won't no turning back. "Me and Talisha got shit to do in the morning and I ain't fucking 'round with you niggas all night Ghost," I lied.

"What the fuck ever, nigga. You rode with me remember? You can't go nowhere until I'm ready to bounce."

Tonight was the first time I've been to Forbidden City since Milk bought the club. I heard that the nigga was doing bad when he came home from prison a few years ago, but from the looks of things it appeared as if Milk is definitely on the come up.

"Yo', man, the VIP room is straight to the back up the stairs," Ghost pointed as he hollered over the music that was blaring through the speakers. "Tone and Rick already back there. I'm getting ready to go holla' at Shorty." He titled his head, signaling to the girl walking toward us.

"A'ight," I slapped hands with him. I turned around and almost bumped into the one person I didn't want to see tonight. Milk.

"What the fuck is you doing in here, nigga?" he stepped to me.

"Look man," I put my hands up, "I ain't got no beef with you, Milk. I don't know what the fuck Juju told you, bu-"

"Juju?" Milk tore his face up. "What the fuck do he got to do with anything? You ain't got amnesia mothafucka' and neither do I."

"Look, a few of my niggas throwing me a bachelor party tonight in VIP. I don't want no trouble man. I ain't in the streets like that no more, so let that shit go, man." Milk looked around the club with an ignorant smirk on his face and then back to me.

"You got one of two choices." He put one hand behind his back. "You can walk the fuck out that same door you just came in or you can get carried the fuck out that same door you just came in. It's up to you."

Let me get the fuck out of this club before "*til' death do us part*" becomes my fate tonight.

# Enter Me, Clear Me!

Rochelle is trying her best to push me to the brink of insanity. She's currently missing in action once again, but this time she left without taking Boom-Boom with her. I've called all of the hospitals in the area, as well as the jails, too, the same way I did when her daddy would pull a disappearing act, and I'm happy to say she wasn't in neither. That's really the only thing I have to be happy about at the present time.

I know your probably wondering why I allow Rochelle to behave the way she does, but the only way that I can explain it to you so that you can understand is I know how Rochelle feels—as well as what she is going through—being a teenage mother. If anyone were to ask me what the hardest job I've ever had was, hands down, I would say it was being a single parent. I know it doesn't excuse Rochelle's behavior, but at this point I really don't know what else to do.

Thank God for Jesus and Shantelle, too, because I don't know what I would do without her. The majority of my clients now come to my house for their hair appointments, and Shantelle really helps me out a lot with Boom-Boom, but I'm still not making as much money as I did at the salon.

It's going to cost me over two thousand dollars to get my car fixed and that's just the body work. I don't know what Rochelle hit but it damaged the CV joints on the driver's side. Two thousand dollars was like two million dollars to me right now, so for the time being I'm back on the bus.

"Hello, how are you doing?" I spoke to the bus driver. "Can I have an all-day pass please?"

The driver never looked up to acknowledge me because she was too busy strolling through her Twitter page on her cell phone, but she did take the time to press the button for me to receive my day-pass. There was hardly anybody on the bus so I was able to get a seat right up front.

"Miss, do you have a cigarette?" a man sitting behind me asked.

"No, I don't smoke," I replied, and turned around in my seat.

"Miss, you got a dollar I can get?" he asked another passenger.

"Yeah, and some sense to go with it. Stop begging mothafucka'. Support your own got damn habit." I turned around to see who she was. "It burns me up to hear a man ask a woman for a cigarette. With ya' begging ass!"

'She did have a point.'

When I turned back around I saw an elderly couple boarding the bus.

"Young lady, how much is a day-pass for senior citizens?" she asked the bus driver.

"A dollar," the driver harshly answered.

"Okay," the woman replied with a smile. "Wilbur?" She turned around to the man standing behind her. "You go ahead and sit down while I dig up this here money."

"You can go ahead and sit down, too, and just pay the fare at the next stop. I ain't got all day to wait on you." The bus driver fastened the doors.

*'Now, that was rude!'*

"Oh, okay then. Come on Wilbur, she said we can pay at the next stop."

"Hurry up I got to move this bus."

The bus driver didn't wait for the couple to find a seat. She immediately pulled out into traffic causing the elderly woman to stumbling into me. I quickly reached out to her to keep her from falling down.

"Oh, baby I'm sorry. Did I hit your head?" she apologized.

"No ma'am, I'm fine. Let me help you to your seat."

"No, I'm alright." She sat down in the seat next to Wilbur and started rummaging through her bag. I saw that she was about to get up again to pay for their fare, so I told her that I would do it for her, because the bus driver was zipping down the road as if she was in a drag race. "That's was very nice of you dear. It's good to know that there are some good young people left in the world. See, Wilbur, there's hope for this generation after all. Thank you." She flashed a warm smile.

"You don't have to thank me," I said, as I walked back to my seat.

"I'm Rose, and this here is my husband Wilbur. We've been married for sixty-seven years. Yes indeed." She nudged Wilbur on his arm.

"It's nice to meet you Ms. Rose. I'm, Angelle." I reached my hand out to her. "How are you doing today, Mr. Wilber?" He didn't respond.

"He don't hear to good these day," she said in a hushed tone, tapping me on my arm. "Wilbur?" Ms. Rose turned to him and shouted. "Dis' young lady asked how you doing?" Mr. Wilbur nodded his head and smiled. "He don't talk to me either." She leaned toward me. "Especially, when he ain't got his teef' in his mouth. He forgot to put them in dis' morning." She started laughing. "Hell, I reckon I talk enough for the both of us."

"Wow, sixty-seven years. That's a long time," I said in amazement.

"That's just how long we've been married. Wilbur started wooing me when I was fourteen." When Ms. Rose said that, I immediately thought of me and Onion. "You like my shirt?" she pointed. "I got a matching hat to go with it, too." She leaned her head forward. "Me and Wilbur walked from Green Run High School all the way to where the bus picked us up from a few minutes ago just to see President Obama. Ain't that right Wilbur?" she raised her voice again. I glanced over at Mr. Wilbur and he had fallen asleep. He was also wearing an

Obama t-shirt only his was blue and the one Ms. Rose wore was pink.

"I didn't' know the President was coming to Virginia Beach today." I guess I wouldn't know. I don't watch the news or read the newspaper. I was depressed enough.

"He sure did and he touched my hand, too." She held it up. "And I'm never gon' wash dis' hand again either." We both started laughing. "I'm just teasing. But I tell you one thing, our President sure is a good looking man. He's even more handsome in person than he is on TV. Michelle was right there standing beside the President, too, just as a wife should be."

"That's nice Ms. Rose. I'm glad you got to see him," I told her.

"Actually, this was my second time seeing the President. Back in 2008, I saw him when he came to Harbor Park out there in Norfolk. It was cold out there that day, too, but me and Wilbur bundled up and went right on out there." She smiled. "I never thought I would live to see a black President of the United States." She raised her right hand up in the air. "Praise the Lord. I remember back when black folks couldn't vote. Do you vote . . . uh . . . uh . . . what did you say your name was, baby?"

"It's Angelle, and yes I do vote," I lied.

"Good." She patted my knee. "Black folks don't know the struggles we had to go through back in the day just to be able to ride up here in the front of dis' bus. Me and Wilbur marched right long side

Martin Luther King, and I know he don' rolled over in his grave ten times at the mess goin' on in dis' world today." She shook her head. "Black folks out here killing each other and keeping score, don't make no sense do it, Angela?"

*'I didn't have the heart to tell Ms. Rose that wasn't my name.'*

"You're right," I agreed, still thinking about Onion.

"That's why I thanks God every day when I open my eyes in the morning, 'cause I am truly blessed, white hair and all!" She snatched her hat off. "And I ain't gon' dye it either. Dis' here comes from old age and I ain't shamed to say that I'm eighty-six, glory to God." Ms. Rose put both of her hands in the air this time.

"Amen and Hallelujah!" the woman who had just finished cussing the beggar out praised.

"Yes, indeed, I give Him all the glory. Everybody should. Not a soul walking this earth should ever have a thing to complain about or a nasty attitude." Ms. Rose leaned in close to me again. "Like Ms. Thang' up there driving this bus." She tilted her head, signaling to the bus driver. "You hear how she talked to me?"

"Yes ma'am I did," I whispered.

"I was half a hundred before she was even though about. These young people ain't gots' no respect." Ms. Rose turned her lips up. "If she don't like a job she needs to gon' and get her another one. Life is too short to be miserable, but I'm gon' pray for her. We all get sad sometimes 'cause we is human, but you can't stay there too long. Every day is a gift from God."

*'I wish it were that simple.'*

I thought about the conversation I had with Ms. Rose while I waited for Shareese to call me to the back. I jotted down a few things that Ms. Rose shared with me in my notebook just to pass the time. I wondered if Onion and I would still be together right now if he were still alive.

"Angelle, you can come on back." I gathered up my things and followed Shareese to her office. "I'm glad to see you, Angelle." She closed the door behind me. I sat down. "What made you change your mind about your therapy sessions?"

"I don't know." I looked around the room.

"Sure, you do. Tell me what are you feeling at this very moment?"

"Afraid," I admitted.

"Afraid of what?" she prodded

"I got a letter from my bank the other day telling me that they were raising the mortgage on my house."

"How does that make you feel?"

"How would you feel, Shareese, if you were in jeopardy of losing your home?" I asked in a condescending tone.

"I know how I would feel, Angelle, but I want to know how it makes you feel? We're not here to discuss my feelings, these sessions are about you," she countered.

"I'm pissed! I can barely keep up with the payments now," I raised my voice. "The realtor led me to believe that I was under a fixed-rate loan with my lender but come to find out the loan was set up as an adjustable-rate mortgage. The bank has the option of adjusting the rate monthly, quarterly, or annually every three years if they wanted, too."

"Have you thought about selling your house for something less expensive?"

"Now you sound like everybody else," I sighed, "I guess I don't have a choice in the matter now, do I?" I shook my head. "I'm just so sick of everything! Every time I get up on my feet there is always something or someone waiting there to knock me right back down."

"Angelle, I want you to do something before we continue."

"Do what, Shareese? What do you want me to do?" I snapped and folded my arms across my chest.

"I want you to do a breathing exercise," she suggested. "I can tell by your body language that you're feeling a lot of anxiety right now."

"I'm just upset, I'll be alright. Just give me a minute," I told her.

"That's all the more reason for you to do this right now, Angelle," she scooted to the edge of her chair. "I want you to put your hands down by your side. I uncrossed my arms and followed her instructions. "Sit straight up in the chair." I sat up.

"Close your eyes." I closed them. "Now take a deep breath, hold it for five seconds, and then release it. And as you breathe in and out I want you to say this mantra in your head at the same time, 'Enter me, clear me,' and try to relax your muscle."

"What is this supposed to do?"

"Give it a try and you will see."

My first reaction was to throw a temper tantrum like I did in my last session but right about now I'm willing to try anything. I closed my eyes tightly, took a deep breath, and silently chanted to myself, *"Enter me, clear me . . . enter me, clear me . . . enter me, clear me."* I don't know how long it had been before Shareese told me to open my eyes, but I will admit it did have a calming effect on me.

"How do you feel?"

"Better, but breathing in and out is not going to solve my problems."

"Try not to look at this issue with your house as a problem but more as a situation that needs to be resolved."

"A situation, huh?" I smirked. "So I should also look at the money I need to come up with to have my car fixed as a situation, too? How about the fact that my teenage daughter hasn't been home in almost a week, that's situation, too? I've had situations to deal with all of my life, Shareese, and I'm tired! Do you hear me? I'm tired!" I buried my face inside of my hands and started to cry. Shareese came over and sat down next to me.

"It's okay, Angelle." She rubbed my back.

"It's not okay, Shareese," I whined, as I lifted my head. "I'm tired of feeling this way. It makes me feel weak and like a failure. I can't do anything right!" I cried.

"Yes, you can Angelle. You already have. I know coming here today took a lot of courage. At least give yourself credit for that. Here," she said, as she passed me a tissue. "I want to schedule you for two sessions a week instead of just one."

"I can't afford that, Shareese." I wiped my eyes.

"Yes you can because I'm going to wave my fees," she offered. Shareese put her arm around me and my body quickly reacted to her comforting embrace. You would have thought somebody died the way I was carrying on. It has been so long since I allowed anyone to get within hugging distance for fear that I would break down like I was doing at this very moment. "I promise you Angelle, it's going to be okay."

I made another appointment with Shareese for Monday and rushed out of the building to meet my bus.

ᵃ

# Out of State Nu-Nu!

I know this goes against my diet but I had the taste for some Chinese food, Egg Foo Young to be exact, so I had to venture outside of Chesapeake and head uptown to Norfolk for some good old fashion "hood" Chinese food located in Southern Shopping Center of Tidewater Drive. I still haven't gotten over the fact that the City of Norfolk tore down Charley Wong's, another classic hood joint, and replaced it with some damn office buildings.

When me and Ma Pearl moved from Maryland down here to Virginia we lived not too far from Charley Wong's over by Norfolk State University, and since the restaurant was in walking distance of our house I nearly overdose on Charley's famous Beef War Mein. I haven't been able to find any good greasy Chinese food like that ever since it was closed down. I had to cut out all of my fast food binging once I had my gastric by-pass surgery. Believe it or not I used to weigh well over three-hundred pounds, and standing at 5'9—believe me; it was not a good look. But for the most part, I try to eat healthy.

I walked into my apartment and closed the door behind me with my foot because my hands were full.

"Pearline, you up?" I called out to my grandmother as I walked inside of the apartment.

"If I wasn't up all that ruckus you making is enough to wake a corpse. And who the hell are you calling Pearline?" I started laughing.

"That's your name ain't it?" I sat the food down on the table.

"It sure is but not to you. Where you been at all morning, Pudding?"

Ma Pearl was the only one in the family that called me Pudding. She gave me that nick-name when I was a little girl.

"I had a few errands to run, plus I had to pick up your medicine."

"I'm not taking that shit!"

I never waste my time arguing with my grandmother about taking her medicine, because little does she know, she takes her medicine every day. I just crush it up in her food like I am about to do right now.

"Come on Ma Pearl." I pulled out a chair from the kitchen table. "Sit down so you can eat your lunch."

"You went up Norfolk without telling me, Pudding? You could have swung me past Robin's house while you ran your errands."

"You want some soy sauce?" I asked, ignoring her comment about going over to my Aunt Robin's house. Ever since my cousin Tyke came home from prison, and turned Aunt Robin's into drug central, I stopped Ma Pearl from going over there.

"Yeah, I want some soy sauce and I know you heard me, Janea!"

*'Uh oh, she mad now. That's the only time she calls me by my real name.'*

"Ma Pearl, why don't you ask Aunt Robin to come to your house and visit with you sometime? Besides, I only went to Norfolk to get the Chinese food."

I finished mixing the rice and gravy together and sat down at the table next to Ma Pearl. We then joined hands to bless the food.

"Thank you, Heavenly Father, for this food we are about to receive. Father God, I ask that you touch my granddaughter Pudding's heart so that she will take me to go see my youngest daughter Robin. I only have one daughter left precious Lord, now that Pudding's momma is resting peacefully with you. Oh, and God, please bless Pudding with a good man. In Jesus name we pray. Amen." Ma Pearl opened her eyes to my lips pressed together. "Whatchu' got your lips all bent up like that for, Pudding?"

"Because-"

"Wait a minute." Ma Pearl looked at me sternly, interrupting what I was about to say. "I didn't hear your salute."

"Amen. But did you have to add all that extra stuff in there? Pass me the salt and pepper would you please, ma'am?" I said in a sarcastic tone.

"Hold on now, I may be old but I will still go upside your head with my cane." She looked around the room for it. "Sass me again!"

"Ma Pearl, will you please just eat your food? We go through this every time you find out I have been anywhere near Aunt Robin's house."

"You just tell me what's wrong with me wanting to go spend some time with my daughter? You just tell me that!" Ma Pearl raised her voice. "I stay cooped up in this house all the time."

"Every time I ask you to go somewhere, you always say no." I shoveled a spoon full of food into my mouth.

"That's because you want to take me to places I don't want to go," was her rebuttal.

"I'm not going through this with you today Ma Pearl."

The tear glands in her eyes began to glisten. *'Here we go.'*

"I don't know why the good Lord don't just take me now," she said with her arms outstretched.

Before you get sucked into Ma Pearl's Oscar worthy performance and start feeling sorry for my grandmother—don't! She specialized in spur of the moment crying and it was something she did on a daily basis. All I had to do to turn the sprinklers off is to agree to do whatever it was Ma Pearl was throwing a hissy fit.

"Lord, just take me now and put me out my misery."

*'No Lord, take me!'*

"Ma Pearl?"

"Yes, Pudding? You gon' take me over to Robins?" she asked with a smile on her face.

'*See what I mean?*'

"No." I shook my head.

"Oh, Lord Jesus!" she cried out, resuming her theatrical recital. "Just take me in my sleep Lord, I want to go peacefully."

"Ma Pearl, stop saying that. You ain't going anywhere. Now eat your food."

\*\*\*

Now that I've finally gotten Ma Pearl situated, let me tell y'all about the date I had the other night. You know the Nu-Nu I told you I had waiting on me after I left Angelle's house? Okay, so let me tell you. First off, that Nu-Nu turned out to be a fucking "No-No", and I should've known something was up with his ass when he told me to meet him at his friend's apartment instead of his house. Not only did this sorry bastard not have his own place, but he ain't got no car either. The day that I met him he was pushing his homeboy's ride, but that's not what put his ass on the "Fuck-No" list . . . hold on—I'm getting to that. I have to tell you the whole story, because even Rayven couldn't make this bullshit up!

So, after I picked No-No up he suggested that we go back to my place; wrong fucking answer! I do my dirt out in the street, and bringing him back to the house would have only gotten Ma Pearl's hopes up that I had finally met a man worthy enough for her to meet, and she would have set the wedding before he left.

Anyway, No-No then suggested that we go down to the Oceanfront in Virginia Beach and I was like, "Cool. I haven't fucked on the beach in a long time," so I hopped on the interstate and headed down the Beach.

No-No told me the best place to park my car so it wouldn't get towed was down on 58th Street and Pacific. When I turned onto the street I saw that it was very dark and secluded, so I'm thinking me and No-No were about to get out of the car and find a discreet spot to squat on the beach to smash, but then No-No suggested that we stay in the car. So once again, I'm like, "Cool. I ain't fucked in a car since I was sixteen, why not?" Trust me this gets better.

So, we take a few shots of Pinnacle—I keeps a stash of liquor in the trunk of my car—while listening to some music, then No-No starts kissing me all over my neck and his lips were softer than LL Cool J's lips—I can vouch for that 'cause I fucked LL back in '89, don't tell nobody though— and then he moved a little down south and stopped at my titties—which is my spot—and at this point No-No had my pussy jumping; do you hear what I say?

Finally, No-No's hands made their way between my thighs and he quickly discovered, *I didn't have any panties on*—in my Eartha Kitt voice—and as a matter-of-fact, No-No's real name is Marcus, too. So anyway . . . I saw Marcus—no fuck that; I'm still going to call his ass No-No— unzip his pants and when his dick emerged out the hole of his boxer shorts, I told myself I had just hit the "Big Dick" lottery. And when I tell you No-No had one of the prettiest, smoothest, dick I'd ever seen . . . I get mad all over thinking about what happened next.

Me and No-No had the windows so fogged up, I couldn't even see the street lights outside. Then, No-No started talking about how he was going to fuck the shit out of me, while stroking his sweet meat at the same time; and I was ready for it! Next thing I know, this mothafucka' came all over my got damn steering wheel. Yeah, you read it right. So, I screamed on him, "What the fuck?"

His dick ain't come nowhere near my pussy and that mothafucka' was in my car nutting every got damn were. Then No-No had the fucking nerve to say, "This ain't never happened to me before." Shitting me! I put him out of my car with the quickness and left his premature ejaculating ass right there on 58<sup>th</sup> and Pacific. Who the fuck does that?

It's defiantly time for me to take a road trip. The only thing better than some Nu-Nu is some out of state Nu-Nu!

# Earthquake!

"Yeah man, I'll be glad when we say mothafuckin' I do, because Talisha is stressing me out man and breaking my pockets at the same time."

"All women are like that Kabo and after the wedding they find more shit to stress you out about. That's exactly why I'm divorced right now. The wedding ain't so much for the couple who's actually getting married because you really don't have to have all of that extra shit. Women go all out when it comes to weddings to impress other women. If her sister got married at Chrysler Hall, then she gon' get married at the Taj Mahal."

"You right about that man," I agreed. "You want me to trim you down on the top, too, man?"

"Cut all that shit off, Kabo. I was trying to let it grow out so I could twist it up but shit, it's to fucking hot out them doors for all this mothafuckin' hair."

"So, you just want a Caesar?"

"Yeah," he answered.

"Man, what happened to you the other night? By the time I got to Forbidden City, Ghost said you had just left."

"Talisha hurt herself at work so I had to dip," I lied.

"Janea, let me get some of yo' wrap lotion. I'll buy you a bottle when I hit up the supply store later." Janea grabbed the bottle and held it out to Juju. "Thanks bitch. You need anything from the store since I'm going?" Juju asked, and sauntered his way back over to his station. You could hear his shoes click-clacking against the floor over the music playing. *'Sissy ass punk.'*

"Yeah, get me some neutralizer when you go," Janea responded.

"A'ight. Whhhooo. . . chile' turn that up," Juju said, referring to the music. "That's my shit right there. Where all my Twerkers at?" He threw his hands up in the air and started shaking his ass. "Where you get this mix-tape from, Janea?"

"From this nigga I was chillin' with last night. He left it in my car. That shit hot ain't it?"

"Yes, honey. All of Jack-of-Spade's mix-tapes is the shit. Heyyy . . . ehhh . . . ehhh . . ."

This mothafucka' thinks he's a bitch for real. Look at him . . . got his hands on his knees, bent over pumping his ass to Rihanna's song, *Birthday Cake*. I wish y'all could see this shit. In here winding like he a fucking belly dancer.

"*Cake . . . cake . . .cake . . .,*" Juicy Fruit sung along. "*Awww* . . . shit, now! Ri Ri said she gon' make you her bitch!"

"Get it Juju," Janea cheered. "Show them how to do that shit!"

That's the last thing Janea needs to do is encourage his faggot ass. Now this punk is stretched out in a split position humping the floor. I knew Cinderfella ain't have no balls and he just now proved it.

"Y'all don't know nothing 'bout that shit right there!" He got up off the floor and twisted back over to his station. "I won a Twerk contest last week at the Hershey Bar," Juju said.

"Yo' man, that punk act like that all the time?" Rick asked me.

"Man, that ain't shit. For 'bout a month he was walking 'round here wearing suits and ties, now he back to wearing poom-poom shorts and stilettos."

"Kabo, man, how the fuck do you work around his ass all day?"

"Shit, man, Cut N' Curl is in a good location. I been doing a'ight here."

"What's up, Playboy?" Juju walked over to my station. "You want some of this?" He bent over and started Twerking again.

"You better go 'head on with that shit." Rick turned around and looked up at me. "Kabo, you better get him before I fuck his ass up!"

"I'm sure you got a camera phone. Take a picture so it can last longer next time. I'll even strike a pose for you—bam!" Juju burst open the jean vest he had on, with no shirt underneath, exposing his bird chest.

I should take that scarf he has tied around his neck and choke the shit out of him with it. I looked around the shop and all eyes were on us, and everybody was laughing, too.

"Twist yo' ass the fuck away from my station Goldilocks, before I knock the shit out of you!" I put my clippers down.

"Very well Uno, but the next time you and your client wish to speak about Juju, you don't have to chat amongst yourselves. Say that shit to my face." He blew Rick a kiss.

"Mothafucka', I ain't gon' tell yo' ass again to get the fuck from over here be-"

"Before what?" Juju pressed his lips together.

"Before I fuck yo' little ass up!" I started walking toward him and he leaped back over to his station.

"You say you gon' do what?" Juju grabbed the Marcel curlers out of the stove. "Whatchu' say you gon' do, Kato? If you feeling a bit froggy today, well then leap mothafucka'!"

"How's everybody doing?"

I looked over to the door to see who was passing out greetings.

"Man, fuck that butt clenching ass mothafucka,' Kabo," Rick said. "Come on and finish my cut. I got somewhere to be."

"How you doing?" Janea responded to the woman first. I stared Juju down for a hard second before I walked back over to my station.

"I'm doing alright," the heavy set woman answered.

"Ummm . . . hmmm. . . . that's what fuck the I thought, negro! Don't let all this fool you. Jealous bitch!" He turned his attention to the woman who had just come into the shop. "How you doing, how can we help you today?"

"I was just stopping pass to see if anyone want to place an order for dinners tomorrow."

"What kind of dinners?" Janea asked.

"Oh, I got everything. Baked chicken, fish, pork chops, pigs feet, chitterlings. And for the sides, collard greens, macaroni and cheese, candied yams. I cooked everything myself. I got a real good deal on the collards and they are my specialty. I had so many that I couldn't even fit them in my kitchen 'zink.'"

"In yo' 'zink?" Juju wrinkled up his face. "What is a 'zink?'"

"You know, the 'zink in your kitchen," the woman simplified.

"Oh, you meant sink?" Juju corrected her.

"Yeah, that's what I said, in my 'zink. I had so many I had to end up washing those collards in my bathtub."

"Scruuuurrred . . . rewind!" Juju spun his head around to Janea and pointed at the woman with his manicured nails. "Did she just say she washed them damn collard greens in her bathtub?"

Janea started laughing and walked over to the dryer her client was under. "You heard her."

"Uh, nawl . . . no thank you." Buttercup shook his head. "I like smoked ham with my collard greens not a side of toe-jam with a dash of yeast infection. Ummm . . . mmm . . . I'll pass."

As much as I didn't want to I couldn't help but laugh. I'm still gone fuck Juju up one of these days though.

"Now, you didn't have to go there. I cleaned my tub out good before I put those collards in there," the woman testified.

"Before, or after you washed yo' ass in it?" Juju shot back, looking the woman up and down. "But let me see if I can get you some orders. Does anybody in here want to buy any dinners?" Nobody responded.

"I guess not, not after the way you talked about my greens." She pouted.

"You shared that horror story, not me. But now that I think about it, don't you belong to St. Paul AMC?"

"Yeah, why?" She folded her arms across her chest.

"I thought you looked familiar. Don't you have that roaming house down on 29<sup>th</sup> Street, out Park Place?" Juju asked her.

"Yeah, so?" The woman uncrossed her arms and then put her hands on her hips.

"Oh, hell nawl." Juju shook his head again. "Now I really don't want shit you cooked. You might as well hit up the next spot."

"Kiss my ass you fuckin' faggot!" the woman squealed.

"Oh, uhh . . . ahh . . . Aunt Jemammi, if you don't get yo' salmonella selling ass up out of my shop, I'mma' tie yo' ass down to my chair and tame that kitchen running down yo' neck." Juju looked her up and down again. "With yo' ashy ass feet. Scrub them hooves and get some of that dead skin off the next time you decide you want to rock some flip-flops. You need to go somewhere and trade one of those 'zink collard green dinners for some lotion. With all that caked up Tussy deodorant under your arms . . . lady get the hell out my shop!"

The woman looked like she was about to charge at Juju, but instead she stomped out the door while mumbling under her breath.

"Juju, you know you was wrong for that," Janea said, still laughing along with some of the clients.

"No, wrong was coming up in here telling people she cleaned some shit she trying to sell in her bath tub, nasty bitch. She needs to go home and soak them feets' in the 'zink!"

"What if that was yo' momma?" I looked at Juju. "You wouldn't want nobody to talk to yo' momma like that."

"I do not believe anyone was speaking to you, Kojak," Juju said with a neck roll. "Focus on yo' client and stay out of grown folks business."

"Come on now, y'all don't start up again," Janea said.

"Butterfinger, keep running yo' got damn mouth and I'm gon' put my fist through it."

"I don' told you one time Uno, what you can do if you feel some kind of way." Juju twirled around in his chair.

"No!" Janea looked at me, and then to Juju. "We have clients in here. Can't y'all act civilized for one day? Damn!"

An overwhelming quietness followed Janea's statement. Not because of what she said, but because of the vibration that was coming through the floor. Everybody started looking around at one another trying to figure out where it was coming from. I looked at the clippers on my station, and they were vibrating, too. Even the pictures on the walls were swaying from left to right.

"Oh, my God!" Juju jumped out the chair. "Earthquake! Earthquake . . . run for your lives . . . run for your lives!" he shouted.

Sweet Pickles then started running around the shop in circles waving his hands in the air. A jar of cleaning solution spilled over and shit started to fall off of my station.

"Juju, calm your ass down. Everybody go to the backroom and get down on the floor," Janea ordered.

"I don't want to die . . . I don't want to die!" Juju continued with his hysterics', while everyone else—including me—ran toward the backroom.

"Juju, bring your ass own here," I heard Janea say.

"Oh, my God, where is Whitney?"

"I got Whitney, now come on, Juju!" Janea shouted. I was already in the backroom laying on the floor and I could still hear Juju ranting hysterically.

"I'm coming . . . I got to get my MAC make-up bag first and my autographed picture of Whitney Houston!" The faggot finally made his way to the backroom, got down on the floor, only to get up again. "Oh, my goodness, I got to go get my autographed Whitney Houston CD!" Janea pulled him back down the floor.

"Bitch, lay your ass down and take this got damn dog!"

# Kahari!

Once all the commotion from the earthquake calmed down I raced home to check on Ma Pearl. She wasn't answering the house phone or the cell phone I'd gotten for her either. I pray to God she's alright. I don't know what I would do if anything happened to my grandmother. Yeah, she gets on my nerves at times, but I can't imagine my life without her. I've only been in Virginia for ten years and the worst thing that has happened as far as natural disasters were concerned was Hurricane Isabel. Kabo and Juju were still acting like two fools when I left the shop. I'm like Angelle now. I might have to find me another shop to work at, too.

"Ma Pearl?" I threw my purse down on the sofa, and ran down the hallway toward my grandmother's bedroom. "Ma Pearl, are you alright?"

I realized I was talking to myself after I opened her bedroom door. Her bed was made, but her wheelchair was gone. There were some things on the floor that had fallen off the dresser, and the few pictures on the wall were crooked, but other than that everything else in the apartment was still intact.

*'Now, were the hell could she be?'*

I walked down the hallway in a tizzy to go get my cell phone out of my purse. This wasn't the first time my grandmother has left out of the house without me knowing her whereabouts, and I'm sure I know exactly where to find her. I immediately dialed Aunt Robin's number.

"Tyke, is Ma Pearl at your house?"

"Naw, she ain't here. She called earlier this morning to talk to my momma but I ain't seen her. Man, did you feel that earthquake?"

"Yeah. Y'all alright over there?" I looked out of the window to see if she was outside.

"Yeah, we good," he replied.

"Where the hell can she be then? I came home from work to check on her because she wasn't answering the phone. Now I'm worried for real."

"She a'ight, Janea. You check at one of the neighbor's crib?"

"You know what . . . she might be across the hall at Ms. Naomi's apartment. I gotta go." I was about to press end on my cell phone when I heard Tyke calling my name. "What?"

"I'm having an earthquake party later on tonight, come thru. Yo' boy gon' be here." I'm sure he was referring to Terrell, but right about now the last thing on my mind was dick!

"Black people will always find a reason to have a damn party. Hell no, I ain't coming nowhere. I have to find your grandmother." I hung up the phone on him. "A damn earthquake party," I mumbled to myself as I walked toward the front door. I was about to reach for the doorknob when it turned. I then heard voices on the other side of the door and one of them belonged to Ma Pearl.

"I really do appreciate you seeing me home young man. I really do appreciate it. Come on in and let me get you something cold to drink," Ma Pearl said to the man ushering her wheelchair inside of the apartment.

"You don't have to go through all that trouble for me ma'am. I have to hurry up and get back to Newport News before the traffic in the tunnel gets bad."

"Ma Pearl, where have you been?" I stood there with my arms folded tapping my foot on the floor as if I'd just caught my teenage daughter trying to sneak in the house.

"Oh, hey, Pudding," she said as if nothing was wrong. "This here is my granddaughter I was telling you about, Kahari. Ain't she pretty?"

"Yes, ma'am, she sure is." Kahari winked at me. "How you doing?"

I annoyingly waved my hand at him. I was mad as hell and Ma Pearl knew it, too, that's why she was trying to avoid making eye contact with me.

"Do you have any idea how worried I've been about you? Where have you been, Ma Pearl?"

"Now, if I haven't taught you anything, Janea, I've taught you some manners. You know you suppose to speak to folks when they come into your house."

"Hi," I said with a quick head nod. "Do you make a habit out of going around picking up old ladies?"

"Janea," Ma Pearl shouted.

"No, it's alright Ms. Pearline." Kahari sat Ma Pearl's bag down on the floor. "I really have to be going. It was nice to meet you, Pudding."

*'Did he just call me Pudding?'*

"Umm . . . hmm . . . get home safe." I nodded my head at him again.

"I'm so sorry Kahari. I don't know what's gotten into my granddaughter today." Ma Pearl narrowed her eyes at me and said. "She must've fallen down and bumped her head during the earthquake."

"Yeah, and there's about to be another earthquake. Good-bye Kahari," I said and closed the door.

"Now was that really necessary, Janea?" she rolled her eyes at me.

"You still never answered my question as to where you've been. How did this Kahari person end up bringing you home?"

"Pudding, I don't have to call and ask for your permission when I want to leave the house. I'm eighty years old your senior and I go where I please. You didn't have to be so rude to that young man. He was just seeing me home."

"Seeing you home from where?" I barked.

"Hold up now, mind your damn tone!" Ma Pearl raised an eyebrow. "If you must know, I was going downtown," she said in a more relaxed manner.

"I figured that. Ma Pearl it's not safe for you to be taking the bus all the way uptown by yourself. How many times do I have to tell you that?"

"That's the point. You can't tell me nothing, 'cause if I want to go visit my daughter then that's what I will do!"

"You still haven't answered my question as to how you ended up with Kahari, Ma Pearl."

"I was at the bus stop when the ground started shaking and he was coming from across the street. You really should call him and apologize for the way you showed your tail Pudding."

"And how would I do that? Furthermore, why would I do that?"

"Well, it just so happen I forgot that talk box thing you bought for me at home and he let me use his talk box to call you. I couldn't remember your talk box number so I called home to reach you. His number should be on that thing that shows you who's ringing your phone."

"Now is not the time for none of your match-making Ma Pearl, you're not slick. You had me worried sick about you." I sat down on the sofa next to my grandmother's wheelchair.

"I'm sorry Pudding. If it makes you feel any better for now on I won't leave out this house again without letting you know first," she sincerely said. "I promise."

There was a knock at the door. I walked over to the door and opened it. I was Kahari.

"Your grandma dropped this outside," he handed Ma Pearl's wallet to me.

"Thank you. And look," I'm sorry for snapping on you the way I did a few minutes ago. I went into panic mode when I came home and Ma Pearl wasn't here."

"I understand, but just know there are still some good people out here in the world. Not everybody out here trying to get over."

"You don't have to stand out in the hallway, suga', come on in and sit down for a spell."

"I can't right now Ms. Pearline, maybe some other time. I'm gon' be late for my client if I don't get on the other side of the water."

"Kahari is a personal trainer Pudding," she mentioned, "can't you tell? Just look at him," she tapped me on the leg with her cane. "Didn't you say something about getting a personal trainer, Pudding? All that Chinese food you've been eating lately is starting to show." She snickered. Kahari started laughing, too.

"Ma Pearl?" I looked at her.

"I'm just saying," she hunched her shoulders.

"Thanks again for seeing my grandmother home," I smiled, and closed the door.

Kahari was the perfect candidate for the Nu-Nu list, but the fact that he knows where I live and Ma Pearl, too, automatically moves him to the Fuck-No list . . . however, Ma Pearl won't lying when she said he had a nice body and he's cute. I might have to make an exception to the rule just this one time. Let me go check the caller ID.

# Rise!

"I often wonder if I'll ever get married."

"How would you feel if you didn't get married," Shareese asked.

"Incomplete."

"Why did you choose the word incomplete?"

"I don't know." I sat back in the chair. "That was the first word that came to mind. Isn't that what all woman want, to be in a committed relationship with someone? You're married, aren't you?"

"No, I'm not," she answered. I looked over to the picture on her desk.

"That isn't your family in that picture over there?" I pointed.

"Yes it is. That's my brother and his children."

"Oh, I thought that was your husband and kids," I said after glancing at the picture again. "I guess I just assumed he was your husband."

"Angelle, sometimes things are not what they appear to be even when you're looking right at it."

"Do you plan on getting married one day?"

"I doubt it," she said.

"Well, that goes back to my original question. Don't all women want to get married someday?"

"Not all women. There are some women who are satisfied with just being in a relationship and have no desires to be married. I'm not saying that there's anything wrong with wanting to be married, but I will say this. Angelle, you have to commit to loving yourself before you can even think of loving someone else."

"What's there to love," I asked rhetorically.

"I'm sure there's at least one thing you love about yourself, Angelle. I want to you think about it for a moment, and then tell me one thing you love about yourself."

I sat in silence and deliberated over Shareese's question. *'What do I love about myself?'* "I can't think of anything," I said. "I guess that says a lot for me, huh?"

"What about your children? What about your grandson?"

"What about them?" I crossed my arms across my chest.

"You love them, right?"

"Yes, I love them." I smiled. "Very much so, but I'm supposed to love them. They're my children."

"Your children came from you didn't they?"

"Yes."

"Your children were brought into this world by you and your grandson is your daughter's offspring, right?" I shook my head in agreement. "Well, that's something to love about yourself right there, because had it not been for you neither of them would be here today."

"I guess you're right," I told her. "I couldn't imagine my life without them."

"I'm sure that if you think about it some more, you will find other reasons to love yourself. I have some homework for you to do and I want you to bring it back with you to your next session."

"Homework?"

"Yes, homework," she repeated. "I'm going to give you homework assignments throughout your therapy sessions."

"Oh, Lord," I sighed. 'I didn't sign up for this.'

"Angelle, in order for you to get better, you have to be willing to do the work."

"Okay . . . okay . . . what's my assignment?"

"I want you to list at least ten things you love about yourself and while you're compiling your list, if any negative thoughts emerge I want you to write them down, too."

"I can't believe you're making me do this," I said, as I reached over and picked up my notebook off the table.

"Angelle, I've noticed that you always have that notebook with you when you come to see me. Do you mind telling why?" I was a little hesitant to reveal what I used the notebook for, and I guess Shareese could sense my hesitancy, because she said, "You don't have to share if you don't want to."

"It's just something I keep with me to write down stuff."

"What kind of stuff?"

"My thoughts."

"So, it's something like a journal?"

"I guess you could call it that," I nonchalantly answered. "Shareese, can I ask you something?"

"You can ask me anything you like."

"Why do you think people are buried underground when they die? Isn't there something else that can be done with our bodies other than being treated like animals?"

"There's always cremation."

"That's even worse."

"Have you been thinking about dying lately, Angelle?"

"I'm always thinking about dying. It's the first thing that comes to mind when I wake up in the morning, and the last thing I think about before I close my eyes at night," I disclosed.

"Do you have thoughts about harming yourself in any way?"

"All of the time."

"May I ask what stopped you?" I looked outside at the cars driving by before I answered.

"Shantelle." I lowered my head and fidgeted with my notebook.

"How was Shantelle able to stop you from committing suicide?"

"She found something I had written in my journal. It wasn't quite finished yet," I half-heartily smiled, "I guess you could say Shantelle put her finishing touches on it for me."

"And what was that?"

"I guess you could call it a poem, or spoken word . . . I don't know." I waved my hands. "I'm not a writer or anything." I shook my head. "It's just something I like to do to take my mind off of things."

"I would love to hear something you've written, Angelle." She smiled.

"It's really nothing," I assured her. "You would probably laugh about it with all of your doctor friends after I leave," I said with a feeble laugh.

"Angelle, remember what I told you the first time you came to see me?" Shareese took off her glasses and then sat them down on the table beside her. "Whatever is said in this room stays in this room. You don't have to be afraid of anything. I'm not here to judge you; I'm here to help you." I blinked back the tears that were about to fall.

"I don't know how to tell anybody what I'm feeling Shareese. I'm embarrassed and ashamed. I've kept my feelings bottled up for so long . . ."

"Well, now is the time to let it out Angelle. We all need someone to cry to. I don't mean that literally, but everyone should have a person to share their feelings with. Let me be that person for you and I promise I'll help you get through this," she took my hand into hers, "I promise you. Now let me here this poem." She sat back in the chair.

"Do you really want to hear it?"

"Absolutely," she said with a reassuring smile.

I opened my notebook, flipped through the pages.

*"Today I fell like fighting—and I know you want to know why.*

*I'm tired of putting on a happy face—just to get by.*

*Some people in this world are so cruel and inconsiderate to others. Three years ago today—somebody killed my lover.*

*If I could create a perfect world—I would.*

*A lot of people really don't know me—I think I'm misunderstood.*

*Why is life so hard? I really don't get the meaning.*

*There has to be more to it than what I'm seeing.*

*Now I'm all out of tears as I stare up at the ceiling.*

*When I'm at a stop light, suicide flows through my mind. If I slam on the gas pedal; I can end it all in no time.*

*I shake that thought off, and proceed with caution. My next suicide thought creeps up without a notion.*

*If I run into a tree, or drive into the water—but then I think; I can't do that, I have a grandson and two daughters.*

*So, I head on home, and retreat to my room—the gun clutched in my hands, ready to end this gloom.*

*My daughter knocks at my door, "Ma are you alright?"*

*I lied and said, "Yes; I'm in the bed for the night."*

*But what my daughter didn't know, that on the other side of the door—her momma was in a fetal position; crying—laying on the floor.*

*Today is the day—today I will finally do it!*

*Because the way I've messed up my life; I don't want to live another minute . . ."*

I stopped reading.

"Is there more?" Shareese asked.

"Shantelle wrote the rest."

"Please finish it. I would love to hear the rest."

"Okay, but can you give me a second?" I covered my face with my hands.

"Take as much time as you need, Angelle." She passed me a tissue.

I cried for well over a minute before I gained my composer. I took a deep breath.

*"But, then in the back of my mind—I hear a calming voice . . .*

*Get up from there my child—this is not your only choice.*

*You see, you are my child—just like everyone else. The devil has gotten to you—and you don't believe in yourself.*

*You are beautiful—no matter what they say. I know you may not have known this—but I've been here everyday*

*So rise my child; fear not anymore. My only son was crucified—someone you all should adore.*

*He gave up his life; so that you could have yours.*

*So waste no more time laying on that cold floor—and rise my child; I have something in store!*

*You just take one step—and I will see that you soar.*

*I give all my children just only one life; don't worry—be happy—one day you too will be a wife. You see, the man that I have for you, I've already chosen. And I will give him to you, as soon as your heart is unfrozen.*

*I was there with you today—at that stop light. I took control of the wheel, so you could make it home tonight. Suicide is not the answer—for my child; it is a sin. And the only thing I want you to do is take a good look within. And see what I see, as your Heavenly Father—and then after today, I hope you will never again wonder.*

*For can't you see, my child—how much I adore? From here on out, when you walk through your front door—leave that cold harsh world out on the other side. For your home is your peace—and I shall continue to provide. Not only for you—but the babies I helped you birth.*

*For my child, I hope you now see—how much you're truly worth. Now rise!"*

I opened my eyes.

"Wow," Shareese exclaimed. "That was very powerful, Angelle. You and Shantelle wrote that?"

"Not on purpose." I wiped my eyes with the tissue. "Had it been Rochelle that read what I had written in my journal she would have loaded the bullets in the gun for me," I smirked. "I just don't understand where I went wrong with her. I've never shown any favoritism between my girls. I don't know what's wrong with her."

"Sometimes when our kids act out, it's a cry for help."

"I thought about that, too, but Rochelle doesn't talk to anybody about anything. I guess that's the one thing she did inherit from me."

"We're going to stop for today. I encourage you to do your homework. I'll see you next week."

# You Want Fame!

I walked into the room barefoot, dressed in a long-sleeved pink fitted leotard, a flowing black tutu skirt, with my cane by my side. Oh, and I have on beige leg warmers, too. I want to make sure I give y'all the full visual.

I stood in the center of the room and looked at everyone individually, as they sat on the floor in an Indian style position.

"You all want to be queens?" I glided my cane in the air. "But guess what?" I took a step forward. "Everybody remembers everything." I narrowed my eyes, zoomed in on Delores, and paused. "You learn something once, and it's yours for life." I slowly walked in between them, as they all looked up at me attentively. "But first you have to become a queen!" I raised my chin. "Now, you may be hot shit where you come from," I said, as I continued to move around the room. "You may even have the best wardrobe this side of the Mason Dixon line, but it doesn't matter." I swiftly turned my attention back to Delores. "Because around here." I paused again. "There's no place for a Prim Madonna or any jealous bitches either!" I raised my voice. "You want to become a queen, you gon' have to work yo' asses off!" I hit the floor with my cane, spun around on the heels of me feet, and then walked at a slow pace back up to the front of the room. "You've got big dreams?" You want fame?" They were all now looking at my backside. "Katora, bitch you're late!" I announced when I heard the door open.

"I'm sorry Juju," she said, and then joined everyone else on the floor. I turned around.

"Well, fame cost!" I scrutinized Katora with my eyes. "Bitch, don't let it happen again!" I pointed at her with my cane. "And right here in this room, is where you jealous bitches start paying. And sweat! That's right, I want to see sweat!" I tapped the floor three times with the cane. "And the better queen you are, the more sweat I'm going to demand. So, if you've never had to fight for anything in your life, I suggest you put your bras and jock straps on, and get ready for round one!" I shot Delores a fierce look. "And mommy and daddy's little sons best to come out swinging. Get up on your feet . . . Up . . . up . . . up . . . hurry up, time is money!" They all quickly rushed to their feet. "Okay, now sit back down."

I've always wanted to do that scene for the TV show, *Fame*. I just love Debbie Allen. I remember when I used to watch that show when I was little. *'Oh, shit, I'm telling my age.'* What I meant to say was, when I bought the TV series on DVD the other day . . . *'I bumped into that guy who came into Cut N' Curl trying to sell those old ass DVD's in Loehmans Plaza Shopping Center.'* I fell in love with

Debbie Allen's character all over again. She was actually the muse that inspired my look today. I'm rocking a curly black wig, too, and I look fabulous!

Every year we have a movie themed Drag Queen competition at the Hershey Bar, and I, along with the club owners, organize the event. Today I'm conducting a "Drag Queen 101" course, because I can't stand to see bitches make a mockery of the craft, and some of these whores in here are a hot ass mess! And they wonder why so much shade is thrown at them when they appear from out of nowhere trying to reign supreme in the clubs, so it's only fitting that I put these bitches in check!

Now, I have the utmost respect for my fellow queen RuPaul, but she really don't have them bitches that come on her show best interest at heart. Just like any other reality show, she's exploiting their asses just to make that paper, and the stupid bitches that participate on the show are beyond clueless. I could teach them a thing or two about *Queendomhood*, but when you're balling on a budget I guess you have to learn how to improvise.

"Okay, the first thing I would like to address is make-up. Now you can't achieve a professional drag look wearing Rite-Aid make-up," I announced, as I sat down on the stool I brought into the room before everyone arrived.

*'I'm always well prepared for a lecture.'*

"Well, where should we get our make-up from, Queen Whitney?" Delores asked.

*'Whitney was my drag name of course'*

"I'm glad you asked that question Delores, but bitch don't interrupt me again." I pointed at her with my cane. "Invest in quality make-up such as MAC, which is the brand I use." I ran my hand down the side of my face. "Also, you can purchase clown make-up at your local costume store, such as Party City. That works well, too."

"Well, what's the difference?" Delores asked.

*'Didn't I just tell this bitch about interrupting me while I'm speaking?'*

"The difference is, if you interrupt me one more time, you will be escorted out this mothafucka'!" I politely voiced to her. "As I was saying," I rolled my eyes at Delores, "no sooner than you start to perform that cheap shit from Rite-Aid will be running down your neck. You can't expect to be taken seriously amongst the rest of the queens if you come into this competition half-stepping. Something else I wish to raise your level of awareness about is wigs. Please follow me." I hopped down off the stool. "I'm going to show you how to achieve a fabulous big-hair look. And F.Y.I., Indian hair is now out and Brazilian hair is in. Follow me please . . . come . . . come!"

I walked over to the table where I had everything already laid out for the demonstration.

"Everything about drag has to be over the top, as well as overly exaggerated." I waited until everyone was gathered around the table before I continued. "The make-up, the wardrobe, the shoes, and most definitely the hair has to be flawless." I looked around to make sure I had everyone's attention. "Delores?"

"Yes, Queen Whitney?" she answered with excitement.

"Please come over here and stand next to me," I told her, "hurry up now . . . come . . . come!" Delores quickly ran to my side.

"Yes, Queen Whitney?" she asked, still beaming with joy.

"I wish to use you as an example of what not to do," I informed her. The smile she wore on her face quickly diminished.

"What's wrong with the way I look, Queen Whitney?" she grimaced.

"Nothing, besides the fact that you look like Aldo, from the movie The Planet of the Apes, with that tired ass lace front wig you have on." I spun her around by her shoulders. "Take a good look at this wig everyone. You will never achieve volume with a lace front wig no matter how much hairspray you use, or how much you tease it. This wig is thirsty as hell, and even if you poured a whole bottle of Crisco oil on it, it would still look dry. Delores?" I patter her back. "You can go back over there and stand with the rest of the jealous bitches, and thank you for being such a good sport." I smiled. Everyone started laughing.

Delores tramped over to where she was sitting on the floor, picked her bag up, and stomped out of the room in a rage.

*'What the hell is her problem? That was a blatant display of jealous bitch activity at its finest. I'm trying to help her ass out!'*

I went on to demonstrate to the rest of the queens-in-training how to combine two wigs together to master the big-hair look. Next, I talked about stage presence, how to handle a last minute wardrobe malfunction, and various other topics. I opened up the floor for Q&A and before I concluded the meeting I collected the fees for next week's session.

*'Don't knock my hustle!'*

Katora—the bitch who was late—asked me to drop her off at the hotel where she was meeting one of her many men. I was going that way to pick Whitney up from the dog groomers, so I told her that I would drop her off but she was going to have to give up some coins for gas.

I've known Katora, a.k.a. Kenny, for over fifteen years. We meet at Hershey Bar which is a gay club located in the Five Points section of Norfolk. We didn't quite mesh well in the beginning, but now that she has reformed her jealous bitch ways we're the best of friends. Looking at Katora, even when she wasn't in drag, people would never know that "she" was really a "he." Katora has the most refined caramel skin which I attributed to her

Puerto Rican roots, and the bitch has more ass than Serena Williams.

"Who the hell is you going to meet up with in the middle of the afternoon, bitch? I thought freaks only came out at night. And click-it or ticket it, bitch!" That was my way of telling her to put on the seatbelt.

"Wheewww . . . bitch, let me tell you." She put the seat-belt on and turned to face me. "Baby boy is fine as shit!" She licked her lips. "Mi papá es sexy y bueno con ese pape," she said in Spanish.

"Bitch, you worse than those yang's in the nail shop. You in America now, speak English!" Katora started laughing.

"I said, my daddy is sexy and he's good with the paper, too," she translated. "And he got a dick on him that would choke a horse," she added.

"You had sex with him already, bitch?"

"Shit, we got it in on the first night."

"Bitch, let me see his pic, 'cause I know you got one."

"No I don't, I just met him. I haven't had a chance to get any photos yet, but I will after today. And why you do that to Delores, Juju?" Katora hit me on my arm. "You know she's sensitive."

"Fuck that jealous bitch!" I fanned my hand at Katora. "She was the main one I was talking to and did you see that shit she had on?

"I think she's improving," she said in Delores's defense.

"Improving how?" I glanced at Katora, and then turned my attention back to the road. "Just because she has fake titties now, don't mean shit. She needs to sit back, watch, learn, and take notes. Oh, and by the way, Mickey said that she needs us to come in tomorrow for a final fitting before the show."

"You late, I already talked to Mickey. I went the other day, and wait until you see my costume," she said. "Let me out right here." Katora pointed to the Star Bucks on the corner.

"I thought you were going to a hotel, bitch?"

"I am." She unhooked the seatbelt. "The hotel is across the street." I looked threw the rear-view mirror. "I'm going to meet him over there."

"Bitch, why you hiding with this man? He's married, ain't he?"

"No, he's not married, Juju. I don't have time to talk to you about it right now, I'm already running late. I'll call you later," she said, opening the passenger-side door. "Smooches!"

*"Wait til' I see her costume. No bitch, wait until all y'all jealous bitches see my costume,"* I mumbled to myself. I got half way up the street when I noticed that Katora had forgotten her cell-phone.

"Now, how this bitch gon' call me later on?" I said aloud.

I made a U-turn and headed back to Star Bucks, but when I pulled up I didn't see her inside. I drove across the street to the La Quinta Inn with the hopes of catching Katora before she went inside the hotel. I circled the parking lot a few times, and I still didn't see her, so I parked and went inside.

"Excuse me?" I tapped on the counter with my nails to get the attendant's attention.

"Yes, can I help you?" the white girl asked.

"I hope so. My sister is staying here and I forgot what room she's in," I lied.

"I'm sorry, but it's against company policy to give out any information," she informed me with a smile.

"Surely, you can bend the rules just this one time."

"I'm sorry." She shook her head. "I can't do that." I looked behind me to see if anyone was listening, and then reached inside of my purse.

"How 'bout I give you a little something for yo' troubles." I placed a dollar on the counter and discreetly slide it toward her. She started laughing.

"I can't take your money, sir," she said, still laughing.

"Well, thanks for nothing." I rudely snatched up my money. "Jealous bitch," I mumbled under my breath.

As I was walking toward the entrance of the hotel, I saw Katora standing in front of the elevators holding hands with a man. I couldn't see his face because they were facing the opposite direction.

"Katora?" I walked toward her. "Bitch, you forgot yo' ph-" They both turned around.

*'What the fuck! Kabo?*

# Public Service Announcement!

What's going on y'all, this Milk. Sorry for not speaking to y'all earlier but this Juju's shit and a nigga ain't want to step on his toes. But anyway . . . If you just know figuring out that Kabo has a little sugar in his tank then you need to pay closer attention to details because all the signs were there since the very beginning. Most people often lash out at those who embody certain traits that they don't like about themselves.

Me and Kabo go way back but it wasn't until I was locked up with the mothafucka' that I found out he was into fudge packing. For y'all short-bus riders—naw, I take that back. I have a newfound respect for people with special needs because of my son, Mj, but anyway . . . fudge packing means fucking niggas up the ass! You'd be surprised at some of the shit that went on behind the prison walls with niggas you may know.

When I first got to the prison, niggas told me that Kabo was running up in punks harder than Elton John, and to be honest I didn't believe that shit at first because I knew that nigga from the streets, until one day I walked in on Kabo in the showers getting his dick sucked by a well-known prison punk name Pancake, which quickly made a believer out of me.

No, Kabo, won't the only one in prison who got down like that, but I used to look up to the nigga and that shit really fucked me up. He's the one who really put me on to the game and we pumped out in the streets together for years until he got knocked. But it won't like the nigga was gon' be locked up for the rest of his life not that it excuses the shit, because real niggas don't get down like that. And this nigga got the nerve to be getting ready to walk down the aisle. That's why he looked at me the way he did that day I brought grown ass up to the shop to get her hair done, and that's also why I escorted the mothafucka' out my club that night. Fuck that nigga!

Now, Juju gets on my fucking nerves to no end, and it ain't no question as to which side his bread is buttered on, but at least he owns his shit. He ain't out here trying to make the world believe that he's something he's not, and he ain't on that down-low shit either.

So, ladies, be mindful of these mothafuckas' coming home from prison, as well as some of these niggas out here on the street; because it's a lot of them out here on the DL. Y'all are good for hunting a nigga down 'bout some child support, so take the time and do some research on the nigga before you start fucking with him. And for y'all single women going to church with the hopes of finding you a man, don't be fooled by the one's that can rattle off a Bible verse like it's their favorite rap song, or even the ones jumping around faking the holy ghost. You see how the shit came out about Eddie Long, don't you?

For those of you ladies that are married, if you start noticing your husband hanging with a new batch of niggas that you ain't never seen before, all of a sudden, that should definitely raise an eyebrow or two. And when he starts wanting to hit that ass more than yo' pussy that's a red flag that shouldn't be ignored.

A'ight, that now concludes my PSA on how to spot a nigga on the down-low. Y'all, be easy.

# The Main Course!

One thing I will agree with Ma Pearl about is the fact that my love for Chinese food is slightly starting to show. I can definitely pinch more than an inch around my waist area, so I decided it was time for me to hit up the gym. I also used that as my excuse to call Kahari. I might as well kill two birds with one stone and allow him to work me out in the gym, and then work him out in the bedroom later on that night, but everything didn't quite work out the way I had planned.

By the time I left One Life Fitness, not only was I not in the mood to fuck anybody, I had to cancel all of the  hair appointments I had scheduled for the next two days, because I was too sore to get out bed. My calves, thighs, ass, and lower-back were on fire, do you hear me? I had to soak in Epson Salt, and rub myself down with some of Ma Pearl's Ben Gay.

After our session, Kahari, lectured me for an hour on the importance of eating healthy and exercising on a daily basis. He told me which foods to stay away from, and which foods were best to eat streamed through one ear, and out the other one until he said, "You can come over to my crib, and I'll show you how to cook the food." Then he had my undivided attention.

I was checking him out, even though he was working the shit out of me, and baaabbbyyy . . . when I tell you that Kahari had a body that would make Idris Elba jealous, it's the God honest truth. Kahari immediately graduated from the Nu-Nu list to the Fuck-a-licious list by the time I had finished a lap on the treadmill. I forced myself out of the bed today, because where there's dick, Janea will make a way! I'm sitting in Kahari's apartment as we speak.

"Did you have trouble finding my place?" Kahari asked.

"Not really," I told him as I looked around, "I don't get over to this side of the water that much, but GPS lead me straight to you. You have a very nice man cave Kahari."

"It ain't much, but its home," he replied, as he rinsed vegetables in the sink.

*'Damn! I wish y'all could see this nigga's ass in these shorts.'*

"This has to be your mother in this picture," I held it up. Kahari turned around to see what I was referring to.

"Yeah, that's my baby right there, but she ain't as cute as me." He grinned.

"Somebody sure does have a big head." I sat the picture back down on the shelf. *'I sure hope he has a big dick to match.'*

"So, I've been told."

"How long have you lived in Virginia?" I asked just to keep the conversation moving.

"I moved here about five years ago."

"Where are you from?"

"New York," he answered. Now that he said that I realized Kahari did have an upstate accent. "Would you like some wine?"

"You're my personal trainer, should I be drinking wine?" I smiled.

"Yeah, you can drink wine just as long as you drink it in moderations, and not every day."

"Well, then I will have some wine only if you're drinking with me." I walked into the kitchen and stood next to Kahari. "That smells good. What are you cooking?"

"Mango grilled fish in butter sauce and a vegetable salad to go along with it. You saved your appetite, didn't you?" He passed me a glass of wine, and then poured some for himself.

"I always have an appetite. What's on the menu for dessert?"

"That's a surprise." Kahari looked at me over his shoulder. "Go sit down and get comfortable," he suggested, "I got this in here."

I walked back into the living room and sat down on the loveseat. I normally don't do this, because this is too much like a date, but I guess I can sit back and relax while he's cooking. Plus, I'm still a little sore.

"How long have you been a personal trainer, Kahari?" I took a sip of my wine.

"For about five years now. I used to be in the entertainment industry when I lived in New York, before I moved down here to Virginia," he shared.

*'Oh, Lord, not another one.'*

"You're a little too old to be an inspiring rapper don't you think?" He started laughing.

"Yeah, I would be if that's what I was trying to do. I'm actually a choreographer."

"Is that right?"

"Yeah, I've been dancing for as long as I can remember. I worked professionally for years and with some well-known people in the industry, too. What kind of dressing do you prefer with your salad, Janea? I got Vinaigrette, or low-fat Ranch?" He held up both bottles.

"Ranch is good. What made you stop dancing and become a personal trainer?"

"I was black-listed after I got into it with an industry heavyweight," he answered. Kahari walked into the living room to refresh my glass of wine. "I still pick up a few gigs here and there, but my goal is to open up my own dance studio here in Virginia. Come on, the food is ready."

I followed Kahari into the dining room where he had the food already spread out on the table. I pulled out a chair and sat down.

"Get up for me, Janea."

"Why, what's wrong?" I looked up at him.

"Just stand up," he repeated. I stood up. "Move over here for a second please."

"Do what?" I gave him a confused look as I stepped to the side.

*'Okay, now I see what he is doing.'*

Kahari pushed the chair back under the table, only to pull it out again. "Now, you can sit down," he said.

"All of that just to pull my chair out for me?

"Girl, sit down," he ordered. *'Who is he talking, to?'* "I'm talking to you," he proclaimed, as if he had read my mind. "I know it ain't too many gentlemen out here, but some of us men still open doors, and pull out chairs," he said with a slight grin on his face.

"If you say so." I sat back down in the chair. "Thank you."

*'I was trying to hurry up and get dinner over with, so we can get to the real main course!'*

"You're welcome."

"This is really good Kahari," I told him after tasting the fish. "You didn't make this. You must've ordered this from a restaurant or something and threw it in the oven before I got here."

"Girl, you crazy, I can burn in the kitchen baby. There ain't nothing I can't make. I lived in a house with my mother, and four sisters, so I had plenty of teachers. The million dollar question is, can you cook?"

"That would be a no." I slightly shook my head. "Ma Pearl does most of the cooking in the house. I do enough to get by, but you'll never catch me slaving over a hot stove."

"I like the way you wear your hair, Janea. I think a lot more sisters should rock the natural look."

"That's coming from somebody with no hair at all," I said, referring to his bald head.

"Oh, that wasn't by choice." Kahari ran his hand across his head. "I took after my father when it came to balding at an early age, so I decided to cut it all off."

"You wear it well." I smiled.

Kahari and I sat at the table for what seemed like hours. The surprise for dessert turned out to be homemade cheesecake—which was to die for—and we also guzzled down another bottle of wine. I saw that it was after twelve when I glanced at the clock on the microwave, and I must admit I was enjoying his hospitality, but it was now time to get down to the business at hand; fucking!

"So why are you single, Janea?"

"Why are you single?" I shot right back at him.

"Can you let your guard down for a little while? I've been doing most of the talking, and you really haven't told me anything about you, Ma."

"Because, there's not much to tell," I told him.

"You seem like you cool people and I would like to get to know you better."

*"How about we get to know each other better in the bedroom,"* I thought to myself. "There really isn't much to get to know."

"I don't believe that," he replied. "Let's go into the den and channel surf to see what's on TV." He stood up. "You're not in a hurry, are you?"

*"Uhhh . . . yeah. In a hurry to get in the bed!'*

"No, not at all."

I followed Kahari into the den, and after ten minutes of doing exactly what he'd suggested—channel surfing—I realized it was up to me to get this show on the road.

"How would you like some more dessert?" I spoke softly into his ear.

"Naw, I'm good. Whatchu' like to watch on TV? I got just about every channel."

"I really don't watch a lot of TV. You can turn it off for real if you want to." I scooted closer to him.

"Let's see what's up with Animal Planet. I love watching that shit."

*'Are you kidding me?'*

"I didn't come over her to watch no damn Animal Planet!" I stood up. "You can do that after I leave."

"I got a nice DVD collection, too. Go 'head and pick something out. They are on the shelf over there." He pointed.

"You can't be serious." I put my hands on my hips. I was becoming beyond pissed, and I'm sure the look on my face expressed it, too.

"What's wrong with you, Janea?" Kahari sat the remote down on the table and stood up in front of me.

"Look, we're both adults. We don't have to play these games."

"What games are you talking about, Shorty?

"This whole cuddle up, satellite surf shit," I voiced. "I didn't come over here for that."

"Janea, when I invited you to my house I had no intentions of having sex with you tonight."

"Boy, please!" I rolled my eyes, and waved my hand at him.

"That was the last thing on my mind, I promise you." he said sincerely.

"Oh, okay I get it now. You play for the other a team, right?" I looked around for my purse.

"No, I'm not gay, Janea." He laughed.

"What the fuck is your problem then?" I crossed my arms.

"I don't have a problem." He sat back down. "Women aren't the only ones who practice the ninety day rule."

"What ninety day rule?"

"Not having sex with someone you meet until at least ninety days," he explained.

"Whoever came up with that bullshit is a damn fool, but I'm sure that applies only to people who are looking to enter into a relationship. That's not on my agenda."

"What's so wrong with being in a relationship? You don't want to ever get married someday?"

"No, not if I can help it. I don't want to spend the rest of my life looking at the same mothafucka' every day."

"Damn, somebody must've really hurt you bad, 'cause you the first woman I ever heard say some shit like that."

"You don't know shit about me!" I waved my index finger at him.

"That's what I'm trying to do. Get to know you Janea."

"Why?" I pressed my lips together.

"Why not?"

"So you're trying to tell me that you wait three months after you meet somebody to have sex with them?"

"To be honest, no, but there still ain't nothing wrong with it."

"Yeah, that's what I thought." I put my purse on my shoulders.

*'Kahari's ass had just been demoted to the Fuck-No list!'*

"Wait a minute, Pudding." He stood back up. "You didn't let me finish. No I may not wait three months, but I sure as hell don't have sex on the first date anymore."

"Who said this was a date? And don't call me that!" I yelled.

"Okay, I'm sorry. Whatever you want to call what we did tonight. Can you please just sit down for a minute, and stop all that damn hollering?"

"Why?"

"Fuck it then. You don't have too. I ain't gon' make you stay if you ready to leave," he said, and sat back down on the chair. It was obvious that Kahari and I were not going to be doing the Hump dance tonight, but I sat back down beside him anyway. "Look, all I'm saying is that niggas learn from their mistakes, too."

"And what did you learn?" I asked sarcastically.

"I used to be around a lot of women being in the industry, and I had my share of them, too, but after a while that shit gets old. Trust me when I tell you that when you've had one pussy, you've had them all. It's that emotional connection that you share with a person that makes the art of making love special. Not just banging each other out for five or six minutes then you gone."

"Six minutes. Is that all you got in you?"

"That was a figure of speech, Janea." Kahari sounded aggravated.

"Did I hit a nerve?" I smiled at him.

"Nope. I'mma' let you talk your shit for right now. I plan on showing you how I get down, just not tonight."

"Oh, so suddenly you have something to show me?"

"Yeah." He kissed me on the lips. "In ninety days." I hit him playfully on his arm. "I'm just messing with you."

"Kahari, I don't do relationships. That's not my style."

"I heard you the first time." He kissed me again. "Turn around this way and put your feet up here," he patted his thighs.

"For what?" I looked at him funny.

"Man, what kind of niggas you been dealing with? Put your feet up here, Janea, damn!" I stretched my legs out on his lap. Kahari then took off my shoes, and began to massage my feet. "I can tell by the way you're walking that you are sore as shit."

"I can't even lie, the back of my thighs are killing me," I admitted.

"That's to be expected, but I'mma' get you right. Sit back and try to relax. I'll wake you up if you fall asleep."

And that's exactly what I did. Kahari woke me up around three o'clock so I could go home. Our quote, unquote "date" ended up with a few more kisses, and a hug. I don't know y'all . . . I guess I can slide him over to the "We'll-See" list I just made up. I left Kahari's house with "blue" pussy. That's equivalent to the blue balls men get, so I guess I will have to whip out my B.O.B.—battery operated boyfriend—when I get home.

# You Want To Be Grown!

I had another session with Shareese this afternoon, and I can honestly say I'm starting to feel a little better. I haven't decided what I'm going to do as far as my house was concerned, but I did sell my car to the mechanic who was working on it, and I got a nice deal, too. Shareese told me about a friend of hers who was selling her car, so I met with her after my session, and took it for a test drive. It appeared to be in good condition, but I don't know the first thing about cars. All I've ever done was put gas in it and go. I asked the guy I sold my car to if he would take a look at it for me and if everything goes well, I should have the car by Friday.

I treated myself to a Spa day, and I stopped at Chipotle for lunch. Then I went to the Barnes and Noble to get the books Shareese suggested I read in our session earlier today. *The Power of Now,* by Eckhart Tolle, and *The Several Spiritual Laws of Success,* by Deepak Chopra. We also talked more in depth about meditation, so I picked up a few audio books, too.

I never schedule any clients on the same day as my therapy sessions, and since Shantelle took Boom-Boom to Water Country with the church today, I have the house to myself for a little while;

or so I thought. Rochelle must've come home sometime after I left the house this morning, because as I walked up the stairs I could hear music coming from her bedroom—no wait a minute, the music was coming from my bedroom. When I reached the door, and turned the knob, I found that it was locked.

"Rochelle, open this damn door! What the hell are you doing in my room anyway?" I banged on the door again. "Rochelle!" I could hear something banging up against the wall from the other side of the door. *'What the hell is that?'* I took a step back, and with every bit of strength I could muster up, I repeatedly kicked my bedroom door until it was open. "What the fuck? If you don't get the hell out of my house you'd better!" I hollered. "Now, I know you have lost your damn mind!" I looked at Rochelle. The boy that was on top of her two seconds ago had jumped up out of the bed.

"Aaron, you don't have to go nowhere," Rochelle told him, as she sat up in the bed. "We can just take this into my room."

"Ma'am, I'm sorry. Rochelle told me this was her house," he proclaimed, as he put his clothes on. "Shorty you ain't right," He shook his head at Rochelle. "I'm sorry, ma'am, I'm really sorry."

"Just get the hell out!" I pointed toward the door. Rochelle laid back on the bed wearing nothing but a smirk on her face. "You think this shit is funny?" I stood over top of her.

"As a matter of fact I do." She started laughing. Aaron was now down the stairs and out the front door.

"Oh, really?" I folded my hands across my chest. "You know I've had just about enough of your shit, Rochelle. Get the fuck up out of my bed before I hurt you!"

"You ain't gon' do shit to me!" she hollered back. "I do what the fuck I want to do. This is my daddy's house." Before I knew it I had lunged on top of her and pinned her down on the bed. "Get off of me bitch," she screamed, as she wrestled to get out of the hold I had her in.

"No, I'mma' show you a bitch!"

The fact that Rochelle was my child instantly escaped my mind, because I attacked her like she was a woman on the street. I thought about every disrespectful word that she had said to me in the past, and I was beating her ass for the ones to come in the future. Rochelle was able to free herself from the grip I had on her, and threw a punch that landed on the side of my chin, but her next attempt was blocked by my arm followed by a series of punches of my own. We rolled off the bed and onto the floor, and the battle royal continued.

"Ma, what are y'all doing?" Shantelle yelled, appearing out of nowhere. "Stop," she said, attempting to pull us apart. "Ma, please. Rochelle, y'all stop fighting." It was only when I heard Boom-Boom crying that I stopped hitting Rochelle.

"Get out of my house right now Rochelle!" I hollered, as I tried to catch my breath.

"Bitch, you busted my lip," she screamed.

"I'm going to do more than that to you if you don't get out of my sight right now!"

"What is going on?" Shantelle jumped in between us. "Ma, what happened?" she cried.

"Shantelle, take Boom-Boom in your room," I told her.

"No!" Rochelle reached for him. "I'm taking him with me! Fuck this house!" I grabbed Rochelle by the arm and pushed her naked body out of my bedroom.

"You not taking him anywhere," I protested. "You want to be grown, then carry your ass out there and be grown. Javari is staying here with me!"

"Oh, we gon' see about that," Rochelle said, holding her lip. "I'll be back to get my son!"

"Ma-"

I put my hand up in the air.

"Shantelle, I said take your nephew in the room, please!"

Shantelle picked up Boom-Boom and left out of my bedroom. I stood in the hallway to make sure Rochelle didn't try and take him with her, and once she left the house, I went back into my bedroom and closed the door. My room looked like a hurricane had just swept through it and I was in no hurry to tackle the mess. I sat down in the middle of my floor, crossed my legs, clasped my hands together, and closed my eyes.

*"Enter me . . . clear me . . . enter me . . . clear me . . . enter me . . ."* I chanted to myself.

When I opened my eyes again it was dark outside. I got up from off of the floor, walked into my bathroom, and turned on the water to take a shower. I was just about to step into the bathtub when I heard a knock at my bedroom door.

"Ma?"

"I'm getting ready to get in the shower, Shantelle, I'll be out in a minute."

"Ma, the police are here."

# When You Do Shit in the Dark!

Kabo has all of a sudden come down with flu, according to Talisha, and he hasn't been to work for the last three days. I started to tell her that ain't all his ass has come down with. I wish you could have seen his face when he turned around and saw that it was me. Could have bought his ass with two pennies, and I loved every second of it. I must say though, Kabo flew under my "*gaydar*", but when you do shit in the dark, it will always find its way to the light.

Men like Kabo will do everything possible to protect their "dirty little secret" and I refuse to get myself caught up in the drama and bust him out to Talisha. Not that I agree with what he's doing, but I have to protect myself, too, and that nigga would kill me. I just hope and pray that Talisha realizes what's going on before she marries his ass. Either way, he's not going to be able to keep up his charade forever.

"What's up with you, bitch?" I asked Janea.

"Whatchu' talking about, Juju?"

"You been quiet all morning," I told her. She started laughing.

"Why something has to be up with me?"

"Where yo' ass been for the last two days?"

"I swear you nosey," she said, still laughing.

"Shit!" I looked down at my feet. "If you have to break a toe nail, does it have to be the big toe? Fucks yo' whole toe game up!"

"Calm down Juju. Just go to the nail shop and get an acrylic toe nail," Janea suggested.

"Fuck what you heard." I started rummaging through my drawers. "I'm getting ready to glue this bitch back on. Me and Whitney just got our damn toes done yesterday."

"You closing up shop early today ain't you?" Janea asked.

"As a matter of fact I am. I have to go for a final fitting for my costume."

"Costume for what," Janea asked. "How does your scalp feel, Teresa?"

"I'm alright," her client answered.

"Okay, let me know if it starts to burn. Juju?"

"What bitch?" I was now working on my toe.

"Whatchu' going to get fitted for, bitch?" Janea repeated her question.

"For the show coming up at Hershey Bar in a few weeks, you wanna buy a ticket?"

"What kind of show is it, Juju?" Precious asked.

That's right; I ain't even told you the latest. Well, Precious is working back at Cut N' Curl, now that she sees the grass is not always greener across the street. I told the jealous bitch that the first time one of her clients showed up to the shop to get their hair done, and she didn't show up for work, then she didn't have to worry about coming back.

"A movie themed show," I answered.

"Who you gon' be, Juju?" Janea asked. I wrinkled up my face.

"Bitch, is you gon' buy a ticket or not?"

"You know I am, and watch your damn mouth before I squirt your ass with this Pump it Up." She held up the hair spray.

"Bitch, I wish you would. You get a drop of that shit on my outfit, and it's gon' be me and you."

"Who you gon' be Juju, Prince?" Janea's client asked.

"Hell nawl! That mothafucka' owes me five dollars." The girls started laughing. "I have something else in mind that's going to upstage all 'dem jealous bitches. That's why I have to hurry up and get out of here before I'm late."

"I want a ticket, too," Precious bellowed.

"You ain't got no damn money, Precious. Shut up."

"Yes I do, and I'm coming, too."

"Whatchu' gon' do bitch, pry yo' ankle bracelet off for the evening?" I teased her. "Matter fact . . ." I looked around. "Where's my damn purse."

"You ain't right, Juju." Precious laughed.

A white boy walked in the shop with an Edible Arrangement uniform on, carrying the most scrumptious looking fruit bouquet.

"You must be looking for me." I signaled to him with my hand. "Y'all jealous bitches need to get you a man like Mike," I rejoiced, as I walked toward him. "But why the hell would he send me some fruit? I told Mike 'bout all this organic shit."

"Is your name, Janea?" he asked.

"Hell no!" I stopped dead in my tracks.

"I'm Janea," she told him, and licked her tongue at me.

"Well, then, this is for you." He handed the fruit bouquet to Janea.

"Thank you. I'll be right back, Teresa, let me go put this in the refrigerator," she told her client.

"I hope you choke on that cantaloupe," I told her as she walked pass me toward the backroom. "And make sure you save me some, bitch! Okay, I'm out this piece. Janea, don't forget to turn the alarm on."

"I gotchu'. Come on Teresa so I can wash your hair."

"Oh, thank goodness!" Ramona came bursting through the door. "Juju, you have to fix my hair for me. You're not getting ready to leave are you?"

"Ahh . . . uhh . . . Ramona, I ain't fuckin' with yo' ass today," I put my purse on my shoulder. "Yeah, I'm getting ready to leave."

"Come on Juju, my tracks are loose," she wined.

"Bitch, I just did yo' hair yesterday." I put my hands on my hips.

"I know. I went to a cook out after I left and the sun melted my tracks." She put her hands on her head.

"Sucks to be you," I chimed. "Call me tomorrow and I'll try to squeeze you in." I told her and walked toward the door. "Oh, shit. I almost forgot my baby. *Twww . . . twww . . .*" I signaled for Whitney, "Mommy almost forgot you." I walked back over to my station to get Whitney's carry-on bag.

"I thought you were bullshitting when you said you got Whitney's toes done Juju," Janea said. "Lord, I really don' seen it all." She laughed.

"That's right, I sure did. Ain't that right Whitney?" I rubbed noses with her.

"Ewww . . . Juju." Precious made a face. "How can you rub your nose on that thing?"

"Bitch, it ain't no different than you rubbing yo' damn nose up against a nigga's sweaty ass balls when they swinging in yo' face. I laugh and I joke, but don't you say nothing else 'bout my baby," I straightened her.

"Juju, you really not gon' fix my hair?" Ramona pleaded.

"Close yo' eyes and count to ten, and I'll think about it." I told her, and to my surprise the dumb bitch actually did it. "Okay, now keep them closed," I said, as I walked toward the door, "no peeping now," I opened the door, "okay, now open yo' eyes, and go buy a clue, Blue!"

***

"Open this door bitch!" I banged on Katora's apartment door with an open hand. "I know you're in there, bitch open this damn door!" When she didn't come to the door, I pulled out my cell phone and dialed her number.

"Hello?"

"Katora, I know you hear me out here knocking. Come let me in before I huff and puff, and blow this bitch down!"

"Okay, here I come," she replied in a sullen tone.

I must've heard four different locks turn before the door was finally opened and I immediately made my way inside with Whitney in my arms.

"Turn some lights on in this mothafucka', or open the windows." I twitched my nose. "It smells closed up in here." Katora closed the door. "Well, this apartment is a lot better than that mud-hut you were living in out in Ocean View." I looked around. Katora walked away with her head down. "Bitch what's wrong with you?" A loud thud came from the apartment upstairs and scared the shit out of me. "What the fuck are they doing up there?" I followed Katora into her bedroom.

"I don't know," she said, as she lay down on the bed facing the wall.

"Bitch, what the fuck is wrong with you?" I asked for a second time. "Katora?" I nudged her leg. I sensed that she was trying to avoid making eye contact with me.

"I don't feel good," she mumbled.

I put Whitney down on the floor.

"Turn around and look at me bitch."

"Look at you for what, Juju?"

"Bitch, turn around!" I tugged on her shoulder. "*Ummm . . . hmmm . . .* that's what I thought. Kabo did this to you didn't he?"

"I don't want to talk about it Juju, so would you please leave me alone?" She turned her back to me again.

"I guess not, as swollen as yo' lips are. Did you go to the hospital, Katora?"

"Go to the hospital for what?

I got up off the bed and walked across the hall to the bathroom to find something to put on her face. I then went into the kitchen and got some ice out of the freezer for the swelling. As I was breaking the ice cubes up in the ice tray, I heard what sounded like a herd of elephants running up the stairs in the hallway on their way to the upstairs apartment, and Whitney started barking.

"I know baby. Your Aunt Katora lives in the hood." I walked back to Katora's bedroom. "Sit up and put this on your eye." I handed her the ice wrapped up in a hand towel. I examined her face again to determine if she was going to need any stiches. Naw . . . this bitch will live.

*Thump . . .*

I looked up at the ceiling.

"Thanks, Juju." She held the ice-pack up to her face.

"Kabo did this to you because of me didn't he?"

*Thump . . .*

I looked up at the ceiling again and rolled my eyes.

"And he said if either one of us said anything to anybody that he was going to kill us."

"Katora, leave that ignor-"

*Thump . . . thump . . . thump . . .*

"Lawd, have mercy!" I hollered up at the ceiling. "But anyway . . ." I was about to make clear to Katora all the reasons she needed to leave Kabo's ass the fuck alone when I heard Whitney barking again. "That's it!"

"Juju, where are you going?" Katora quickly got up out of the bed and followed me.

"Upstairs to have a word with yo' neighbors!" I opened the front door. "No, Whitney, you stay right here. Mommy will be back in just a minute," I told my angel, and proceeded out of the door.

"Juju, don't go up there. I have to live here when you're gone!" Katora shouted. I ignored her cries as I pranced up the stairs in route to apartment C. This shit don't make no damn sense! I banged on the metal door with as much force as I did when I was knocking on Katora's door.

"Who is it?"

"If you'll open the door I will tell you who it is," I responded. The door opened and a knotty-haired little girl emerged. "I need to speak to the man or the woman of the house, so would you be so kind as to go get them."

"Hold on," she said, and closed the door in my face. "Daaaddddyyyy . . ." she hollered. "Some lady at the door wanna' see you."

*'Some lady? I guess I should take that as a compliment.'*

"What's up?" the man asked, after opening the door.

"My friend is not feeling well and she needs to get some rest, which she simply cannot do with all of the noise coming from up here."

"I'm sorry, my kids can get a little rowdy at times-"

I put my hand up inches away from his face so he would stop talking.

"I didn't ask you for your damn life's story. You need to get better control of Bae-Bae kids, and make them sit they asses down somewhere," I stated.

"No, now hold on . . ."

"Oh, ain't no hold on Harpo," I smacked my lips. "Just reduce the noise or I will be forced to take this matter to the rental office."

"Who the fuck is you calling, Harpo?" he hollered.

"You!" I exclaimed, looking him up and down, "and by the way, your performance in the Color Purple was excellent."

"Now, see, I was trying to be civil with yo' punk ass. I pay rent just like er'body else in this building and my kids can jump up and down all damn day if they won't to." He took a step closer to me. "What the fuck you gon' do about it?"

"How 'bout I just do this?" I clapped my hands together and flashed him and award winning smile. "Why don't I put a call into the police department and let them know that there are some people up in apartment C smoking on some Keisha. Oh, yes, I can smell the weed and yo' black soup coolers," I said, referring to his lips, "is another dead giveaway that you hit the chronic on a daily basis," I tilted my head to the side, and put my hands on my hips.

"A'ight, man, shit! Y'all stop jumping." He closed the door in my face. I walked back downstairs to Katora's apartment. Come to think of it, I should have bought a dime bag from him while I was up there.

"Juju, I can't believe you did that. Now what if he comes down her fucking with me later on after you leave?"

"He ain't gon' do shit!" I waved my hand. "Now back to you." I sat down on the sofa. "There ain't no trade in this world worth getting fucked up over, especially not Kabo's black ass."

"But, I love him, Juju."

"Bitch, tell me tomorrow!" I crossed my legs. "Do you love being black and blue?"

"That's not funny."

"I'm not trying to be funny. Katora, you look worse than Rhianna did after Chris Brown fucked her up. Let that shit go. You had no business fucking with him in the first place. It's not like you didn't know who the fuck he was," I told her. "Talking 'bout you love him. I should have known you were up to something when you told me to drop you off at Starbucks instead of the hotel." I reached over and picked up my purse when I heard my cell phone ringing. I didn't recognize the number but I answered it anyway. "Speak! What? You where? Shut the fuck up! I'm on my way bitch."

"Who was that?" Katora asked

"Noneyo'." I stood up to leave.

"Who is Noneyo', Juju?" she asked with a puzzling look on her face.

"None of yo' business. Keep that ice on yo' face, bitch. Come on, Whitney."

# Rikers Island!

"Excuse me, sir," I said, trying to get Deputy Blanding's attention. I could see his name tag from where I was sitting on the bench.

"Yes," he answered, never looking my way.

"Is it possible I could use the restroom? I've held if for as long as I could.

"It's the first door on your right," he motioned with his head.

"Thank you." I smiled. I walked the short distance to the first door on the right per Deputy Blanding's instructions, opened the door, and turned on the light. "Oh, my God," I said aloud. The restroom was filthy and it reeked of urine. The commode looked like it had not been scrubbed ever, and there was no toilet paper, paper towels, or soap either. I walked back to the deputy's station. "Excuse me again, Deputy Blanding, but there isn't any toilet paper or soap in the restroom."

"That's because people clog the toilet up with it so we took it out," he said.

"Well what about soap then?"

"We took that out, too." He smiled.

"Well, do you at least have any hand sanitizer?"

"Look, this ain't no Holiday Inn. Either you're going to use the toilet or go sit your ass back down!"

"That's okay, I'll wait."

I turned around and walked back over to the concrete bench and sat down. I don't understand how Onion used to come in and out of the place. I've only been here for four hours and I'm scared straight, because this is not for me.

"Angelle Turner?"

"I'm right here." I looked around but I didn't see the person that had just called my name.

"Go around the corner to see the magistrate," the deputy advised. I did what he said.

"Hi, how are you doing? I'm Angelle Turner."

"Have a seat," she said. I sat down on the metal stool. "Have you ever been arrested before?'

"No, I haven't."

"Are you employed?"

"Yes, I'm self-employed."

"Can you afford an attorney?"

"Not at the present time I cannot. See what had happened was . . ." I began to explain before she cut me off.

"Save it for your court date." She waved her hand at me. "You're going to be released on your personal recognizance, but you will have to appear in court first thing Monday morning, is that understood?"

"Yes."

"You can go back over to the wait area and have a seat. You'll be called momentarily."

Deputy Blanding finally gave me permission to make a phone call. I tried calling Janea's cell phone first but I didn't get an answer, and the last person I was going to call to pick me up was my mother. I'm sure Rochelle has given her and earful by now. I only had one other option left. After placing my call I went back over to the bench and sat down. A few minutes later I was led into another room by Deputy Blanding to get finger printed, have my mug shot taken along with two other people.

"You're free to leave," the woman who had just taken my picture announced. "Go over to those double doors and wait for me to activate the buzzer."

*'Thank you, Jesus!'*

Once I got outside I looked around in the parking lot to see if I saw his truck.

"I'm over here bitch," Juju shouted, waving his hands up in the air as he held Whitney.

It has been a couple of months since I've seen or heard from Juju since our blow out that day, and even though Juju can be a pain in everybody's ass at times, he was truly a sight for sore eyes.

*"That's the sound of the man . . . working on chain . . . gang . . . That's the sound of the man . . . working on the chain . . . gang . . ."* Juju sung in a deep voice. I see nothing has changed about him not one bit.

"It's not funny Juju." I started laughing. I opened the passenger side door to his truck and got inside.

"Yousa' damn lie it ain't funny bitch!" he said as he strapped Whitney down in her car seat. "How the hell did you catch a domestic violence charge, Angelle?" Juju started up the truck.

"I came home and caught Rochelle in my bed with some boy and I lost it," I told him.

"Click it or ticket it, honey. I'd put on my seat belt if I were you. Yo' ass just got out of Riker's Island, you should be trying to obey all laws from here on out." I started laughing again. "Now listen," he flipped his wrist forward, "I already got some t-shirts on order but the only thing is Lil' Wayne's picture is on the front of them. So what I'm gon' do is just cross out his name. So instead of it saying free Weezy F. Baby, it will read, free Angelle. Whatchu' think about that?" By now I laughing hysterically.

"Something is seriously wrong with you, Juju. I know I'm not going to be able to live this down for the rest of my life. Please don't tell anybody about me getting arrested," I said getting serious.

"Very well then," he agreed. "Did they feed you bread and water?"

"No. I wasn't down here long enough for that. I was starting to think I was going to be in the dreadful place until Monday morning listening to some of the people talk."

"You did the right thing, Angelle. You should have whipped Rochelle's ass a long time ago. I know I don't have any chirren' myself to speak on other than Whitney, but I would have done the same thing, too. I can't believe Rochelle actually took a warrant out on you though. You should go home and beat the hell out of her ass again." I looked over at Juju.

"I should, shouldn't I?" I tapped Juju on his arm and we both started laughing again.

For some strange reason I am not upset about everything that happened today. No, I'm not going to make a habit out of beating up my children and going to jail, but It's really not effecting me the same way it would have a couple of weeks ago.

"So when are you gon' bring yo' ass back to the shop, bitch?" Juju looked at me out of the corner of his eye.

"Do you really want me to come back?"

"I don't do this too often but I can admit when I'm wrong. I may have displayed a few jealous bitch tendencies but you know I love you Angelle, and I would never do anything to hurt you," he said while batting his eyelashes. "I'm sorry, bitch." Juju made a sad face.

"Aww . . . Juju, you are going to make me cry." I reached over to give him a hug, "I'm sorry, too."

"Okay, so now that we are bitches again, are you going to come to my show at the Hershey Bar in a few weeks?"

"What kind of show is it?"

"It's a drag queen competition. Janea and Precious are coming?"

"Precious? Where did you see her at?"

"She's working back at Cut N' Curl now."

"Wow." I started laughing thinking about Janea. She cannot stand Precious.

"I know, right? I'm waiting for them two bitches to get into it. So are you going to come to the show or not, bitch?"

"Sure, why not?"

"Are you coming back to work tomorrow?"

"No, I have to go down to the courthouse on Monday to see what I have to do to get custody of Javari. I don't trust Rochelle to take care of him."

Juju treated me out to dinner and then took me home and to my surprise, Rochelle and Boom-Boom were in the living room watching TV. I didn't say anything to her and she didn't say anything to me. I changed the sheets on my bed after I got out of the shower and then began reading *The Power of Now,* until I drifted off to sleep.

# Dip Low!

"Hey, Kabo," Angelle said cheerfully.

"What's up?" I walked over to my station and sat my bag of clippers down.

"Are you feeling better?" she asked. "Juju told me you were sick."

"I'm good," I told her. I saw Juju walking from the sink area out of the corner of my eye. "You back?"

"Yeah, I am," she smiled. "It's almost time for the big day ain't it? Are you getting nervous?"

"A little bit," I told her.

"Well, well, well . . . welcome back, Diego," Juju said with a smile. "So happy you could join us today," he said, as he sauntered over to his station. I didn't respond.

"Juju, have you talked to Janea this morning?" Angelle asked.

"Yeah, I talked to that bitch. She ain't coming in today," he told her.

"She's not sick too, is she?" Angelle asked.

"She probably got a dick stuck in her throat," Precious chimed in.

"Well, I guess I'll put some music on," Juju said. "Angelle do you like R. Kelly?"

"Yeah, why?" she asked.

"Okay, that will be the first CD we listen to. Let me know if any of you have any more request." Angelle slightly chuckled.

"Oh, you're a DJ now, Juju?"

"Today I am," he answered, and looked at me with a devious grin on his face.

Juju's first selection was R. Kelly's song, *Down Low* followed by the *Trapped In The Closet* saga, and next up after that was Lil' John and the Eastside Boys' song, *Get Low*. It was apparent that Twinkie was playing all of that shit just to fuck with me.

A'ight, before y'all go forming any opinions about me at least listen to what I have to say first. When I first got locked up I didn't have anybody on the outside looking out for me—as much shit as I did for niggas out on the street—and once I got shipped to a prison in Kentucky, I was really out back, so I made a hustle out. There are actually niggas in prison that will pay you to let them suck you off, and guards too. When it was almost time for me to get out I was transferred to The Berg, and I kept my hustle going, but I only fucked with niggas that were going to be locked up for the rest of their lives. That way I never had to worry about the shit getting back to the streets.

I did run up in two or three punks a few times, but I was always fully protected and never have I been on the receiving end. I ain't apart of no "secret society" of down-low niggas either—I do all my shit by my lonesome—but I can appreciate a fem-queen every now and again. I could never see myself waking up to a nigga in the morning. As a matter-of-fact, I don't even want to see another dick. That's why I never allowed Katora, or any other queen, to get fully naked in front of me. It was alright for them to expose their titties—if they had fake ones—and sometimes I will sneak-a-peek at a neatly trimmed bush, but the dick had to be tucked away so I couldn't see it.

I don't dip-low often—that's how I referred to the lifestyle—and it's not like I'm gay or anything. I'm a man in every sense of the word. If I never got down with another queen again it would be cool with me, because I really do love Talisha and I don't want to risk her finding out.

Now it's really time for me to get up out of Cut N' Curl before I have to fuck Juju up for running his mouth!

# Grown & Sexy!

"Thanks for calling Cut N' Curl, Janea speaking, how can I help you?"

"Hi, I've been trying to reach Juju on his cell phone. Is he available," the caller asked.

"No, Juju won't be in today," I told her. "Can I take a message?"

"I'll just call back tomorrow, thanks," she said before hanging up. I sat the cordless phone back down on the receiver and didn't make it to the sink area before the phone rang again.

"Get that for me, Kabo, I have to wash this perm out of Trina's hair."

"Cut N' Curl," he answered the phone in an agitated tone. "Naw, he ain't here . . . I don't know . . . I don't take messages," Kabo said to the caller. "Call back tomorrow." He hung up the phone. "Man, why Skittles ain't tell his clients that he won't gon' be here today? Shit, phone ringing every five minutes for his ass. I ain't no damn secretary!"

"Where is Juju?" Precious asked.

"He's getting ready for his show in a few days," Angelle answered.

"I told Juju to remind me," Precious responded.

"I can't believe y'all going to that fag club to see a bunch of faggots dressed up like women," Kabo interjected.

"I've been to a gay club before and I had myself a ball," Precious said. "There's nothing wrong with it Kabo, stop being so closed-minded. I've been to strip clubs, too, and I'm not gay."

"Now, the strip clubs is a totally different story," Kabo replied. "I would pay good money to see two women going at it on stage." He slapped hands with his client Tony.

"How does Talisha feel about you going to strip clubs, Kabo?" Angelle questioned.

"What do you mean how does she feel?" Kabo looked down at his client. "She don't know that I be going to the clubs," he started laughing.

"And what she don't know won't hurt her. Ain't that right, man?" Tony added.

"You betta' bet it. A'ight, man, I'm finished." He passed Tony a hand mirror. He examined his haircut, and then passed the mirror back to Kabo.

"Here you go." He handed Kabo a twenty.

"Come on Trina." I followed her back to my station and turned the stove on. "Kabo, why don't you just ask Talisha to go to the strip club with you?" I started combing through Trina's hair.

"Before or after she cusses my ass out?" Kabo joked.

"Why would Talisha want to go to a strip club, Janea?" Angelle looked at me with a confused face.

"Why not?" Precious put her two-cent in. "Would you go to a strip club if your man asked you to?"

"Naw, I can't roll with you on that one Precious." Angelle laughed.

"Shit, y'all women are crazy." Precious shook her head, "I don't see what the big deal is anyway. If y'all go together then y'all gon' go home together. I guarantee he gon' tear your ass up when you get home, too!"

"I'll pass." Trina laughed. "I don't mind if my husband goes to a strip club, just as long as he don't do nothing he ain't got no business doing."

"And how the hell would you know if he did do something he ain't got no business doing?" Precious asked.

"She won't know," Kabo answered for her. "The strip club ain't no place for y'all women to be at anyway. Damn, can't niggas have anything without y'all trying to take that over, too?"

"Why do you go to strip clubs, Tony?" Angelle asked.

"Shit, I go there to get my dick sucked!" Tony answered, slapping hands with Kabo again.

"Tony, aren't you married?" Precious winked at him.

"Yeah, I'm married but my old lady ain't into giving head," he answered.

"Man, is you crazy?" Kabo asked. "I'll be damned if I'm gon' get down on one knee and propose if she won't get down on two."

"That's why I go to the strip clubs." Tony laughed.

"Y'all niggas are a trip," I said.

"Why you say that, Janea?" Kabo asked and sat down in Juju's chair.

"Nothing, I'm going to keep my thoughts to myself," I told him. I was really talking about Tony. I don't blame his wife for not sucking his little meat.

"Naw Janea, go 'head," Kabo insisted. "You got me curious now."

"Y'all niggas act like y'all are always pleasing to a woman. Instead of going to a strip club some of y'all need to be taking a class on how to fuck and eat pussy right." I looked at Tony. Angelle and Precious fell out laughing.

"Whatchu' mean by that?" Tony asked with his face balled up.

*'A hit dog will holler.'*

"Just what I said," I rolled my neck at Tony. "Hold your head down for me Trina. There needs to be a strip club that women can go to like an emergency room after a botched fuck!" Kabo joined in on the laughter. I think he knew I was speaking on Tony by experience.

"My wife don't have any complaints." Tony put his hand between his legs.

"A lot of women don't have any complaints, they just suffer in silence. *'Like his damn wife is doing.' You* would be surprised how many women are out here faking orgasms." The shop telephone was now ringing again. I looked over at Kabo who was shaking his head.

"Hell naw, yo' turn, Angelle. Get the phone." Angelle answered the phone and it must've been for her because she walked toward the backroom.

"I've never faked an orgasm," Precious said. "I'll tell a nigga quick to get the fuck from off of me."

"A'ight, Kabo." Tony stood up. "I'm gone man."

"A'ight, man. You coming to my bachelor party next weekend ain't you?"

"You know it. Where's it gon' be at?" Tony asked.

"I don't know yet. Keith putting it together, but I'll hit you up before Friday."

"A'ight, man." He slapped Kabo's hand. "Y'all be good."

"You, too, Tony," I winked my eye at him. Tony had a look of disgust on his face. I know he was pissed off with me because of what I said, but I didn't care. He walked toward the door and never looked back.

"Janea, you ain't shit," Kabo started laughing.

"Why, what I do?" I winked.

* * *

"Ma Pearl?" I closed the front door behind me. "What in the world." I looked around the apartment. The lights where off and the room was lit up with candles. "What is she up to?" I said aloud. "Ma Pearl?" I sat my purse down on the couch.

"Ma Pearl is next door," Kahari answered.

"What are you doing here?" I smiled at him. "And why is my grandmother next door this time of night?"

"Stop asking so many questions and come over here and sit down," he told me.

"What is all this?" I asked, referring to the food spread out on the dining room table.

"Dinner," he answered, and then pulled out a chair for me to sit down. "I figured you would be hungry after working so late today." I sat down.

"You figured right. The holidays can get very hectic but you didn't have to do all this for me," I said still smiling. "How did you get Ma Pearl to go over Ms. Naomi's house?"

"Girl, please, your grandmother loves me." Kahari sat a plate of food down in front of me, and then kissed me on my cheek.

"I've been thinking about you all day." He sat down in the chair across from me.

"Is that so?"

"That is so." He smiled. "I always think about you when we're not together."

"You're not going to eat?"

"Naw, I ate with Ma Pearl before she went next door."

"I bet she didn't even take her medicine." I stood up.

"Yes she did. I crushed it up in her food like you told me you did. Now sit back down and eat your food."

"Ummm, this is good. I see fish isn't your only specialty," I said referring to the steak. It was so tender I didn't have to cut it with a knife.

"I told you I can burn in the kitchen girl, whatchu' thought I was playing?"

"Naw, I believe you because this baked potato is on point, too. This was really nice of you. Thank you. Nobody, well, no man has ever done anything like this for me before.

"You're welcome, baby. I've really enjoyed the time we have been spending together lately."

"You have?"

"Haven't you?"

"I guess so. I know you didn't make these string beans," I said. I wanted to change the subject. "Ma Pearl cooked them, didn't she?"

"Nope, I cooked everything. So, whatchu' got going on next weekend?"

"I don't have any plans, why what's up?" I wiped my mouth with a napkin as I got up from the table.

"Where are you going?"

"To get me something to drink," I told him. "Is that alright?"

"Sit down I'll get it for you. My bad. I forgot to take the wine out of the freezer." I sat back down and Kahari got up and walked into the kitchen. "Since you don't have any plans tomorrow night, why don't you come somewhere with me?" He sat a glass down in front of me and filled it with wine.

"Go where with you?"

"Remember I told you that I coached football?" I nodded my head yes. "We're having a dance to raise money for the team at the Long Shoreman Hall." He sat back down.

"Thank you, but no thank you. I don't do kid parties." I took a sip of wine.

"Girl, it ain't no kid party. This is for the grown and sexy folks, so you'll fit right in."

# Queen of the Night!

"Where you on your way to?" Rochelle asked, as she stood in the doorway of my bedroom. "Whatchu' got a date or something?"

"No," I answered, looking at Rochelle through the mirror. We've hardly said two words to each other since I went "medieval" on her. We went to court the other day and I guess you could say she had a change of heart, because she told the judge that she was the one who initiated the fight between us, and the case was dismissed. "I'm hanging out with Janea and Precious for a little while tonight.

"Oh," she said barely about a whisper. "Your hair looks nice." I had to turn around to make sure I was looking at the right twin.

"Thank you. Where's Boom-Boom?" I turned back around to finish applying my make-up. Rochelle walked over and sat down on my bed.

"I just put him to bed."

"Why so early? You usually let him stay up all times of the night."

"I know. I guess I'm trying to work on my parenting skills." She stood back up. "Ma?"

"What?"

"Why don't you let me pick out an outfit for you to wear tonight," Rochelle offered. I looked down at the dress I selected for the evening.

"What's wrong with what I have on?"

"Nothing, if you were sixty years old it would be perfect." We both started laughing.

"That's mean Rochelle," I looked at myself in the full length mirror on the wall. I guess it was kind of dated. It's been so long since I have bought any new clothes so I really didn't have much to choose from.

"Take that dress off. I'll be right back," she said and left out of my room.

"Rochelle, don't bring no hooker gear to wear tonight," I hollered out to her as I started to undress.

"This is not hooker gear." She passed me the dress after returning to my room.

"It's really cute, but I don't have the shape to wear this, Rochelle."

"Ma, yes you do. You just never wear anything to show your shape. Turn around so I can zip you up." I put the dress on and turned around. "See, this color goes good with your skin tone. It matches your hazel eyes, too." I turned side-ways to get a glimpse at the dress from behind.

"You don't think that it's cut too low in the back?"

"No, Ma, it looks really good on you. Just because you're a grandmother doesn't mean you have to dress like one. Ma, you're still young. Don't hide your curves, flaunt them."

"Well, what kind of shoes should I wear with it?"

"I got that covered. Now sit down on the bed and let me touch up your make-up."

I don't know what has come over Rochelle but whatever it was it made me feel good. Maybe Janea was right. I should have cuffed her up a long time ago had I known it would make her act like she had some sense.

"That heel is too high, Rochelle, I might break my neck in these."

"No you won't. They go good with that dress." She sat back down on my bed.

"Look Rochelle, I-"

"Ma, you don't have to say it. I already know," she cut me off. "I'm the one who should be apologizing to you."

"Oh, I wasn't going to apologize, because you asked for that."

"I know." She lowered her head.

"Rochelle, is there anything you want to talk to me about? I know that we've had a rocky relationship for a while now but you can come to me about anything. You know I love you, right?"

"Yeah, Ma, I'm just not ready to talk about it right now," she said with tears in her eyes.

"So, there is something wrong? You're not pregnant again are you?"

"No, Ma, I'm not pregnant."

"Well, what is it then, Rochelle?"

"Ma, go have you a good time, and stop worrying about me. I'm going to be alright," she smiled.

* * *

I left the house feeling like a million-dollar bill. Janea offered to come and pick me up but I told her I would just meet up with her and Precious at the club now that I was driving again. When I pulled into Hershey Bar's parking lot, she and Precious was standing by Janea's car waiting for me.

"I still can't believe your ass came out the house tonight," Janea said as we walked toward the club entrance. "That dress looks really good on you Angelle, but you picked the wrong club to wear it to." She laughed.

"Thanks. Rochelle picked it out for me, and she did my make-up, too." I smiled.

"Umph, that ass whipping you put on her must've moved mountains," Janea said. I stopped walking.

"Juju told you?"

"Naw, he ain't tell me shit. Girl please, you know I gets' the scoop. Virginia ain't but so big. Come on,. Janea pulled me by the arm.

"Can one of you pay my way inside the club?" Precious asked. "All I have is an ATM card."

"Hell no," Janea quickly answered. "You do this shit all the time. Every time I go out with you, you claim you either forgot your ATM card, wallet, or your money. Precious your ass is always trying to get over on somebody."

"Naw, for real Janea, here go my ATM card right here." She held it up.

"Bitch, I'm sure they got an ATM machine in here."

"You know what I'm not even sure if I have enough money on my card come to think of it. Angelle, can I hold twenty until we get back to work tomorrow?"

"Don't give her ass shit, Angelle!" Janea said as she opened the door so we could go inside. "I'm telling you she does this shit all the time. That's why I stopped going out with her ass."

"Come on, y'all." I looked at Janea, and then to Precious. "We came out to have a good time and enjoy ourselves. Here Precious," I reached inside of my purse. "Here," I handed her a twenty dollar bill. "If you don't pay me back then you don't have to worry about me loaning you any more money ever again."

"Girl, don't listen to Janea. I promise you I will give it back to you tomorrow."

"Don't say I didn't tell you how this bitch gets down, Angelle."

"Janea, let me hold twenty so I can buy me some drinks."

"Bitch, you better swallow your spit!"

"Janea?" I laughed, shaking my head at the same time. "Girl, you is crazy."

"Y'all come on before it gets to crowded," Janea said. We paid the cover charge and followed Janea through the crowd in search of an empty table. "I see Mike over there," Janea pointed.

"Where?" I looked around.

"Right there by the stage," she answered. Precious and I followed Janea over to the table.

"Ladies." Mike stood up to greet us. "All of you look beautiful."

"Thank you, Mike." I sat down. "This is a really good table. We're right in front of the stage."

"Juju reserved this table for us. You see the card, don't you?" Mike pointed and laughed.

"Look at this shit." Janea held the card up. "This table is reserved for Juju. No jealous bitches allowed." Janea sat the card back down in the center of the table. "Juju needs to stop his shit." She giggled.

"Can I get you ladies anything from the bar," Mike offered.

Precious was the first to give Mike her drink request and I looked over to Janea who was rolling her eyes. I tapped her on the shoulder and said, "Be nice." Mike left the table and made his way over to the bar.

This was the first time I'd ever been inside of a gay club and it was not at all what I had expected. I assumed there would be shirt-less men walking around wearing black bowties and tight bootie shorts grinding all over each other, but it was nothing like that at all. The atmosphere was really nice. I looked around at the diverse group of people and wondered which ones were gay.

"Janea, do you think that guy over there is gay?" I signaled with my head.

"All day long," she replied without hesitation.

"He's really cute." I leaned closer to her so she could hear me over the music. "What about him over there?" Janea followed my eyes.

"Yep," she confirmed.

"Wow, It's no wonder so many woman are single. All the cute ones are gay,. I laughed. "What about him right there?"

"That's a girl."

"Really?" I looked again. "She's cute, too. I would have never guessed she was a girl." Janea had a look of surprise on her face.

"Umph, let me find out," she said.

"I'm just saying." I laughed.

*"There's some hoes in this house . . . there's some hoes in this house . . ."*

"Janea, they're playing your song," Precious said, trying to be funny.

"Bitch fuck you!" Janea bucked.

"Y'all don't start," I told them. "Y'all are worse than Juju and Kabo."

Mike returned with our drinks and sat them down in front of us, and then he and Janea got lost on the dance floor, while Precious and I table danced in our seats. We had a few female admirers offer us some drinks, but I didn't want to give anyone the wrong impression, so I declined. Precious, on the other hand, didn't seem to mind at all. She's now on her third shot of tequila.

The DJ announced that the show was about to begin and for everyone to take their seats. Mike and Janea made their way back to the table and the lights were dimmed. An exact replica of Nicki Minaj was now on the stage wearing a long flowing Cleopatra pink wig, hot pink tights, and a pink bikini top. To tell you the truth, she looked better than the real Nicki Minaj if you ask me.

"The Hershey Bar would like to thank you all for coming out tonight," Nicki announced, as the crowd roared with applause. "And do we have a treat for you tonight. Ladies and gentleman, show your love for . . . Appolonia Six!"

The song, *Sex Shooter* was now playing, and the stage curtain opened to reveal three women standing in front of a metal black cage.

"That's Juju's friend Katora in the middle." Mike pointed. "Isn't she beautiful?"

"What? That is not a dude!" she hollered.

"She looks just like Appolonia." I elbowed Janea. "Doesn't she?"

"She damn sure does and those other two looked just like the girls in the group, too," Janea agreed.

Every detail of the ladies outfit's matched the ones Appolonia Six wore in the movie *Purple Rain*, and the crowd was now on their feet cheering the trio on. The next act to grace the stage were from the movie *Sparkle*, and by the time they finished giving the audience something they could feel, I was in total awe of all the performances thus far. After a brief intermission, the dance floor was cleared, and the lights were dimmed once again.

"I think my baby is up next," Mike said.

"Go, Juju!" I hollered with excitement and stood up.

"Sit your ass down, Angelle. He ain't even on stage yet!" Janea pulled me by my arm.

"Oh," I giggled. I sat back down in my chair and looked around to see if anyone was watching me. I guess that was some of the alcohol screaming for Juju, too.

As the curtain slowly opened there were various images of Whitney Houston everywhere. *The Bodyguard* movie . . . *The Preacher's Wife* . . . oh, and the song, *I'm Every Woman* music video. Fog rose up from the floor and a spotlight zoomed in on the middle of the screen showing a silhouette of a person. I knew then it was Juju. It was so quiet in the club that you could hear a pin drop when all of a sudden the paper was ripped into shreds and the figure behind the paper screen emerged. It was Whitney!

"*I've got that stuff that you want . . . I've got the thing that you need . . . I've got more than enough . . . to make you drop to your knees . . . 'cause I'm the queen of the night . . . the queen of the night . . . oh yeah . . . oh yeah . . . oh yeah . . . yeah. . ."*

"Do that shit Juju!" Janea stood up and shouted. "Do that shit!" The crowd rumbled with applause and whistles, as the spotlight followed Juju's every move.

"That's my baby!" Mike hollered out. I thought he was about to run up on stage.

I am so amazed at how much Juju looked like Whitney from the *Queen Of The Night* music video, and the way he owned the stage was flawless. Juju was a carbon copy of Whitney from head-to-toe. From the crown he wore on his head to the knee-high black stiletto boots—everything was on point! And to think I was about to change my mind about coming out tonight.

Juju won the competition of course and after he thanked all of the jealous bitches across the world for his trophy, he joined us at our table and we had a ball. This was definitely a *"girl's"* night out!

# The Way Somebody Loves You!

Ever since the first time I went to Kahari's house for dinner we have been spending a lot of time together and believe it or not we still haven't had sex. I told him that I would go to the dance with him tonight, but I'm starting to have second thoughts. I don't think I am ready for public appearances as a couple yet.

Well, I've told y'all all of my business up until this point, so I might as well tell you everything. I met this guy through a friend of mine, oh, I would say about twelve years ago, right before me and Ma Pearl moved down here to Virginia, but we didn't meet face-to-face until a year after we first met.

Derrick was in the military and he was stationed in California at the time. There wasn't any Skype or ooVoo shit, like we have now, so we mostly corresponded through letters and the telephone. I was plus-sized, at the time, and I never really had a serious relationship until I met Derrick. Men would often tell me that I had a cute face to be so heavy, so you can imagine what my self-esteem was like back then.

Derrick told me that he liked a woman with a little meat on their bones and he made me feel good about myself. He found out six-months into the relationship that he going to be stationed in Georgia the following year and I was so excited, because that meant he would be a little closer to me. I flew out to California a few times to visit Derrick, and for a minute I was ready to pack up all of my shit and move out there with him, but I knew Ma Pearl wasn't going to want to move across the country. Derrick and I both agreed that we would make the move to Georgia together, but needless to say, that never happened.

One weekend, I decided I to surprise Derrick with a visit and when I arrived in California; the surprise was on me. I don't know where she was the times I visited Derrick before, but when I went to his house I was greeted by Derrick's wife. Actually, they'd been married for five years. I was devastated to say the least, and I made a vow to myself then that I would never let a man hurt me like that again.

Once I had my surgery I had men coming out of the woodwork trying to get with me. That's what was good about moving to Virginia, it was a fresh start for me. Nobody knew me here as "fat" Janea.

I don't know . . . . should I go y'all? Okay, let me call Kahari and tell him I'll meet him there.

***

"How are you doing?" I spoke to the man at the door who was collecting the tickets. "Kahari was supposed to have left a ticket up here for me."

"Are you, Janea?"

"Yeah, I'm Janea." I smiled.

"Baby, you can go 'head in. I think he got a table over there in front of the DJ booth." He pointed.

"Okay, thanks."

It has been a while since I've been to the Long Shoreman Hall, but the place still looked the same, and as usual, the woman to men ratio was ten to one in the men's favor. The dance floor was packed and V.I.C's song, *The Wobble* was playing. Kahari was out on the dance floor putting the rest of the folks dancing skills to shame, because he was really throwing down.

"What's up, cuzzo'?" I turned around.

"Whatchu' doing here, Tyke?"

"My stick man son plays for the Wolfpacks so I came to support," he said in a drunken slur. The DJ switched it up and The Gap Band's song, *Outstanding* was now blaring through the speakers. Some people left the dance floor, while others coupled up with one another—including Kahari—and continued to dance. "Who you here with?"

"None of your damn business, I'm grown!" I instantly developed an attitude watching Kahari dance with another woman.

"Terrell over there, you want me to go get him?"

"No, don't bring him over here. I'm here with somebody," I said in a bitter tone.

"Girl, calm yo' ass down I was just fucking with you. Terrell got three, four bitches in here tonight. He don' fucked all of the kids mommas' on the team, he ain't thinking 'bout you."

When Tyke said that I looked over to Kahari and wondered if the woman he was dancing with was a "Team Mom" and had he slept with her. See, that's why I can't do this relationship shit. I don't like feeling jealous of anyone. I sat down at the table. I wasn't sure if it was the one the guy at the door was talking about, but oh well.

"Whatchu' drinking?" Tyke stumbled into me.

"Water." I tilted my head to the side. "Tyke, you don't need nothing else to drink. And get off of me!" I pushed him.

"What the fuck is wrong with you, Janea?"

"Gon' somewhere Tyke." I looked up and saw Kahari walking toward the table.

"What's up, man?" he spoke to my cousin.

"What's up, nigga?" Tyke slapped hands with him. "You from New York ain't you?"

"Yeah, man," Kahari answered.

"You sound like it. You know my mean ass cousin, Janea?" He staggered into Kahari.

"Yeah, I do." Kahari started laughing. "You mind if I steal her for a minute and take her out on the dance floor?"

"Naw, man, go 'head," Tyke replied, still slurring his words. "Janea, get yo' ass up, the nigga say he want to dance with you."

"Boy, go somewhere and sit down," I snapped.

"Baby, what's wrong?" Kahari reached for my hand.

"Nothing," I quickly told him and moved my hand out of reach. Tyke walked away, stumbling into people that were sitting down at their table. I see right now he's going to have to be carried out of here by the end of the night.

"You're not coming out on the dance floor with me tonight?"

"I don't feel like dancing." I turned my head the other way. "I'm sure there are plenty of woman in here for you to choose from. As a matter-of-fact," I stood up, "I have to use the bathroom."

"Janea?"

I never turned around to answer Kahari. I made my way through the crowd toward the ladies restroom. When I saw how many people were waiting in line to use the rest room, I turned around and walked back into the hall and sat down at an empty table in the corner. The hall was at capacity and I couldn't spot Kahari anywhere, but then again I wasn't looking for him. I knew I shouldn't have come here tonight.

"Why, you sitting over here by yourself?" a familiar voice asked. I looked up. It was Terrell.

"Waiting for you?" I stood up. "Come on, let's get out of here." I grabbed Terrell by his hand.

"Hold up, let me go find yo' drunk ass cousin. Stay right here." He tapped me on my ass. When Terrell walked away I saw Kahari walking toward me.

"What are you doing, Janea?" Kahari asked with a disappointed look on his face.

"What do you mean, what am I doing?" I looked at him unsympathetically. "I could ask you the same thing."

"Did I miss something?"

"Naw, but I did," I said, attempting to walk away.

"Janea, come back here." He gently grabbed me by the arm.

"I'm getting ready to leave." I snatched away.

"Leave with who?" He leaned down close to my ear. "That nigga I just saw you over here talking to?"

"Yeah, and you can leave with that bitch you was dancing with." I tried to walk away again, but Kahari was now standing in front of me.

"Where did all of this come from, Janea? I was only dancing with her."

"You don't have to explain shit to me, do you!"

"Come on!" Kahari grabbed me tightly by my wrist.

"Let me go!" He stopped and turned around.

"Janea, don't make me embarrass you and me in here tonight."

It was something about the way Kahari looked at me and the authority in his tone that made me stop resisting. *'What the fuck are you doing, Janea?'*

Kahari held on to my wrist until we reached the dance floor. Freddie Jackson's song, *Have You Ever Loved Somebody* was now playing. I usually don't do slow songs, but I wasn't about to give him a reason to make good on his threat of showing his ass in front of all these people in here. Once we reached the dance floor Kahari put his hands around my waist, pulled me closer to him, and we began to sway to music.

"Baby, don't mess up a good thing because you're scared." I looked up at him.

"Kahari, I-"

"No, let me talk. I'm sorry that the men you've been with in the past have hurt you but that ain't me, Janea. I'm starting to develop some serious feelings for you girl and we could be beautiful together if you would just let it happen. Now, you can leave with that nigga standing over there looking at us." I glanced over his shoulder at Terrell. Kahari placed his hand on my chin and guided my attention back to him. "Or you can come home with me tonight so I can make sweet love to you."

When I looked back over to where Terrell was standing he was gone. Kahari spun me around and now my back was up against his chest. He then wrapped his arms tightly around me, leaned down, and kissed me on my neck. He slowly began to grind up against me and right on queue with the bridge of the song, Kahari sung along with Freddie in my ear.

"...mmm ... I can teach you how to love again ... If you just trust in me ... I can show you things you never seen ... You don't know how much your missing ..."

Kahari was no Terrell when it came to singing, but I give him an A for effort. We spent most of the night on the dance floor and I really had a good time. He introduced me to all of his friends as his "baby" and by the time we left, I had gotten used to my new title. I would tell y'all what happened next once we got back to Kahari's apartment, but this one I think I will keep to myself. After all, you should never tell other women how your man puts it down in the bedroom. I will say this though; it was well worth the wait.

# Just Like Forest Gump!

*Music playing . . .*

*"He fills me up . . . he gives me love . . . more love than I've ever seen . . . He's all I got . . . he's all I got in this word . . . but He's all the man that I need . . ."*

I was so inspired by Juju's performance the other night that I got up this morning and went out and bought Whitney Houston's *Greatest Hits* CD. I wonder who Whitney was thinking about as she sung this song; God maybe? I've heard all of these songs so many times, but I'm starting to see and hear things in a different way than I used to before. Like the song, *The Greatest Love of All.* When I heard the song before I've always associated it with kids for some reason, but as I listened to the words, I realized that the message of the song was about self-love. I get it now.

I'm so glad I didn't stop my sessions with Shareese, because she has helped me in more ways than one. I've gotten pretty good with meditating too. I don't know what tomorrow is going to bring but right now at this very moment, hour, minute, and second—I'm okay.

I was resting on the floor looking up at the cracks in the ceiling. This house was slowly, but surely, falling apart. I've already had to replace the heating and cooling system, the tile in the kitchen, because of leaking pipes in the floor, and the insulation in the attic. I'm starting to wonder if it's even worth keeping.

I got up from off of the floor and sat down in a chair next to the window. I wonder how it is possible for birds to be able to withstand the heat, but humans have heat strokes. If birds can take it, then why can't we? I sometimes wished I was a bird. I love the way that they glide through the sky so graceful and free. Even the baby birds try their best to keep up with the momma bird. That question brought fourth more questions. How do trees get as tall as they do? Why do the leaves change colors with each season?

The sound of the disk changer brought me out of my trance, and just that fast it had started to rain. I was still gazing out the window when something inside of my head told me to go outside in the rain.

"What?" I questioned my thoughts which quickly repeated, *"Go outside in the rain."* I didn't question it a second time. I hopped up, slipped on the first thing I saw, and grabbed my umbrella.

As I walked out of my house, I saw Ms. Mary, my next door neighbor, walking from her mailbox.

"Good morning Ms. Mary." I waved.

"And good morning to you," she replied with a smile that matched mine. "Where are you on your way to in this rain, Angelle?"

"For a walk around the neighborhood," I told her.

"You picked a bad day to go walking. It's just drizzling now, but it's about to pour down. Look up at them clouds."

"I know Ms. Mary, but something told me to come out here, so here I am." Our conversation was briefly interrupted when Tim, the neighbor across the street, pulled up in his drive-way.

"Umph!" Ms. Mary grunted, and pressed her lips together.

"What's wrong, Ms. Mary?"

"You ever pay attention to all the traffic coming and going from their house?"

"Not really," I said as I tried to hold my umbrella in place. The rain was really beginning to come down now.

"Something ain't right over there just as sure as my name is Mary Jones. All times of the day and night they in and out. I know what they doing, too," she declared.

"What are they doing, Ms. Mary?" I asked, as I tried to contain the laughter that was stirring inside of me. I'm sure she had her speculations about what may have been going on inside my house too before Onion died.

"They over there doing that dope!" she said with conviction. A chuckle escaped out of my mouth, but I quickly suppressed the one behind it when I saw Ms. Mary's serious facial expression.

"You think so?"

"I know so," she answered, along with a head nod. "Well, go 'head and enjoy your walk in the rain. I got some smoked turkey necks on the stove and I don't want them to burn."

"Alright Ms. Mary, I'll see you later."

I decided to walk to the park down the street from my house, and I happened to look down at my selection of clothes. I can imagine what Ms. Mary said under her breath about my ensemble of stripes and solid colors, accented with fuchsia pink flip-flops. I allowed myself to unleash the laughter that I was holding inside thinking about what Ms. Mary said about our neighbors across the street.

There was a cool breeze in the air that came from out of nowhere, and it felt good blowing against my skin even though it was still raining. I didn't try to avoid the puddles of water that splashed against my legs as I walked because the water was warm and soothing. Suddenly, I threw my umbrella into the bushes, lifted my head up toward the sky, and allowed the raindrops to fall all over me. The next thing I knew, just like Forest Gump, I was running!

I was running away from that house. I was running away from the pain. I was running away from hurt. I was running away from: noise, darkness, despair, guilt, and any other negative emotion I have ever felt. I felt free as a bird and I was chasing the wind. I was running toward serenity. I was running toward redemption. I was running toward God! Peace within never felt nearer.

# Black Stallion!

"Hey, Kabo, what are you still doing here?" Angelle asked when he opened the door.

"I'm on my way out right now. Y'all behave yourself, and I don't want no damn strippers in my house either Janea," Kabo laughed and closed the door behind him.

"I can't believe that I let you talk me into coming to Talisha's Bachelorette party, Angelle. You know that bitch don't like me."

"She invited all of us to come. I wonder where Precious is," Angelle looked at her watch.

"If she know like I know she will stay her ass where the fuck she is, 'cause this shit looks boring as hell."

"It's still early, Janea," Angelle reasoned.

"She should have asked me to help organize the party. What kind of Bachelorette party is this? Everybody sitting down like they're at a tea party," I complained. If I had my way I would be over Kahari's house curled up on the sofa, but he's hanging out with the fellas tonight.

"Shhh . . . Janea." Angelle looked around.

"Whatever." I waved my hand at her.

Angelle and I sat down on the couch as I continued to survey my surroundings. Talisha was wearing a tiara on her head and she had a t-shirt on that read "Bride to Be" and every five seconds she was flashing her engagement ring for all to see.

Angelle leaned in close to me. "So, tell me about this guy." I turned my head the other way so she wouldn't see that I was smiling. "Well, I declare. Are you blushing, Janea?"

"No," I told her, still not looking in her direction.

"Have you slept with him yet?"

"None of your business!"

"Lord, have mercy; it's going to snow tomorrow." Angelle slapped her knee and giggled.

"Why you say that?"

"Janea, for as long as I've known you, you have never been tight-lipped when it comes to men. You must really like Kahari." I didn't try to hide the smile that crept up on my face this time.

"I do, Angelle, I like him a lot."

"Okay, we have to toast to this." She stood up.

"Where are you going?"

"To get us some drinks. I'll be right back.

"Hey, Janea, how are you doing?" Talisha asked.

"I'm fine," I replied in a voice as phony as the one she greeted me with. "Congratulations."

"Thank you," she said, sweeping her hair away from her face. *'Bitch, I see your ring.'* "Well, thanks for coming."

"You're welcome." I faked a smile.

"Here you go." Angelle passed me a glass.

"What is this?"

"Vodka and cranberry juice." She sat back down on the couch beside me.

"Ladies, the stripper has finally arrived," Talisha announced.

"*Whoopdy do,*" I mumbled to myself. I think I was the only one in the room who wasn't excited. I've never been into strippers unless he was doing a private show just for me. I looked over at Angelle and even she had a Kool-Aid smile on her face. "What's been up with you lately?"

"What do you mean?"

"Something is different about you all of a sudden. Don't tell me you don' found you a man," I teased her.

"No, I'm just high off life." Angelle went inside of her purse and pulled out a stack of one dollar bills.

"I see you came prepared," I told her.

"I sure did." She fanned herself with the money in her hand.

"Did they have anything good up on that table to eat?" I asked.

"Yeah," she answered.

"A'ight, you enjoy the stripper. I'm going to find me something to grub on. Watch my purse," I handed it to her. "Hi, how are you doing?" I spoke as I passed a girl that looked just like Talisha. She had to be her sister.

I started to go straight for some fried chicken wings, but then I thought about Kahari. I could hear his mouth now telling me that the chicken was a bad food choice, so I opted for the baked chicken instead.

"Are you ladies ready for Black Stallion?" Talisha eagerly asked. The women answered her question with screams of yes, as well as applause. I was still piling food on my plate with my back turned to the crowd. "Hit the music Stesha!"

The lights were dimmed and all of the women were up on their feet. Usher's infamous song, *Little Freak* was now serenading the ladies, and all I could hear were chants of "oohhhsss" and "aaawwwsss" so I figured the stripper had made his way into the living room. When I turned around I saw a man dressed in black chaps with no shirt on, wearing a black cowboy hat, and he also had on a mask that covered his eyes. I made my way back over to where I was sitting beside Angelle, and she too was up on her feet. Talisha was sitting in a chair in the middle of the floor as the stripper made his way over to her.

I was just about to bite down on a piece of celery when I noticed the stripper had a birth-mark on his lower thigh. I sat my plate of food down next to me and stood up. Now that I was able to get a closer look at him I realized it was exactly who I thought it was. Kahari. I walked right up to him and snatched his hat off of his head.

"Janea, what are you doing?" Angelle yelled.

"What the fuck are you doing?" I hollered at Kahari. "You're a stripper now?" I turned around. "Angelle, give me my purse!"

"Janea, wait." Kahari tried to grab my arm.

"Get the fuck off me!" I snatched my purse from Angelle and walked toward the front door.

"Janea, wait. What's wrong?" Angelle followed me. I ignored her and quickly shot out the door.

I was moving so fast I didn't even notice the girl walking up the stairs until I bumped into her and almost knocked her down. It was Juju's friend Katora.

"I'm sorry."

"That's okay, honey. Are you alright?"

"Yeah, I just got to get the fuck out of here."

# You, Me, and He!

I walked into the apartment and stumbled over what looked like a suitcase that was sitting on the floor next to the door.

"What the hell . . . Talisha!" I looked around the apartment it was a complete mess. See, this is way I didn't want her to have her bachelorette party here in the first place. Look at this shit. "Talisha?" I walked down the hallway toward our bedroom. "Talisha, why the fuc-, oh hey Stesha, I didn't know you were still here. Good, you can help clean all this shit up. Is that your bag at the front door? I almost broke my damn neck when I came in."

"Stesha, take this for me," Talisha handed her a carry-on bag. "Wait for me downstairs, I'm coming."

"Wait for you downstairs for what?" I looked at Talisha, and then to her sister. I followed Stesha's cold stares as she walked out of the room. I then noticed that Talisha's clothes were no longer in the closet. "What's going on, Talisha?" I looked at her. I could see that she had been crying, too.

"You fucking bastard!" Talisha twisted her engagement ring off, and then threw it at me. "This mothafuckin' wedding is off!"

"The wedding is off for what? What the hell is going on?" I walked over to her.

"Don't come near me Kabo!" she backed up. "Don't you ever put your fucking hands on me!" she screamed.

"Baby, what's wrong with you? Why you got yo' shit all packed up? What happened?"

"I'll tell you what happened, your little boyfriend came here tonight that's what happened, you nasty bastard!"

'Boyfriend?'

"Talisha, what the fuck is you talking about? I grabbed her by the arms to try and calm her down.

"Katora, that's who I'm talking about! I thought I was getting ready to go toe-to-toe with a bitch until Angelle told me he was a fucking man!" she continued to scream. My heart began to race.

"I don't know no damn body name Katora, who the fuck is that?" I lied.

"And you gon' stand right in my face and tell me a bold face lie. He showed me the pictures of you in the bed together, Kabo!" She pulled away from me. "I saw them with my own two eyes. Here I was questioning you about bitches and you fucking around with a got damn man!" Talisha walked over to the dresser and frantically pulled the drawers open. "I see women coming into the hospital everyday getting diagnosed with Aids because of nasty mothafuckas' like you!"

"Talisha, I'm telling you it's not what you think. I admit I was wrong for even meeting up with her, but I had no idea it was a dude," I lied again. She didn't respond. "Baby, please listen to me." I walked up behind her.

"Get the fuck away from me! This 'you, me, and he' relationship is over!"

"Now, wait a minute, you gon' listen to what the fuck I got to say!" I hollered, as I grabbed her from behind.

"Let go of my got damn sister mothafucka'!" I turned around and saw Stesha standing in the doorway brandishing a knife. "Come on Talisha," she said as she walked toward me. "I'll come back and get your shit, just come on."

# Combined Session!

"What has changed since the last time I saw you?" Shareese asked.

"Remember when you told me that I needed to tap into the little girl that still lived inside of me?"

"Yes." She nodded.

"Well, the other day I was lying across my bed listening to the neighborhood kids' play outside, but unlike other days their loud screams and laughter didn't bother me. I used to holler out of my bedroom window at them to go to one of the neighborhood parks to play, but I didn't that day."

"What was different that day than any other day you've heard them outside playing?"

"I realized that I used to be jealous of those kids," I chuckled to myself. "I know, it sounds crazy right?"

"No," she disagreed. "Not at all. But why would you use the word jealousy? Usually people are only jealous of someone when the other person has something they wanted or wished for."

"I think deep down I secretly wanted to be outside running around, screaming, jumping, and everything else they were doing without a care in the world, too. I wanted their happiness. I wanted their innocence."

"There's nothing wrong with feeling like that Angelle. You've often said that you feel as if you missed out on your childhood because you had your children at such a young age."

"I know, but for a long time I blamed myself for everything that has ever happened to me. I felt like I brought everything on myself. The depression, getting pregnant when I was only fifteen, hell, even Rochelle getting pregnant at a young age. I put that monkey on my back, too. I just felt like I ruined my life and I could never get it back. I always felt like I was missing out on everything. Almost like there's still a little girl inside of me that needs to come out."

"And how do you feel now?"

"Okay, don't laugh," I blushed. "I wrote a letter to myself that day. Well, not to me," I put my hand on my chest, "but to little Angelle."

"I'm not going to laugh at you Angelle. I think that was a good idea for you to do that. It shows that you are taking charge of your feelings and not just suppressing them. Did you bring the letter with you today?"

"I did." I smiled. "Do you want me to read it to you?"

"Absolutely," she replied. I reached inside of my bag, took out my journal, and then flipped to the page I had written the letter on.

*"Dear little Angelle,*

*The time has come for me to let you go and allow Big Angelle to take it from here. We had a lot of good times and we had a lot of not so good times and our parting is going to be bittersweet. I know there are a lot of things you missed out on because of me and for that I'm sorry. If we could time travel, as Shareese would say, I would go back seventeen years without a second thought, but we can't. I know you had to grow up fast because of the choices I made, and for that I am also sorry. I'm sorry that I allowed people to use you. I'm sorry that I allowed people to abuse you. I want you to know that you did nothing wrong. You will always be a part of me you'll just have a different role from now on. I'm sure you will emerge at times, especially when I see a box of Alexander the Grape or Boston Baked Beans candy when I happen to run across a convenience store that still sells them. I'll be sure to get some and I won't share them with anyone just like you used to do when we were little. I will always love you and I will never allow anyone to hurt you again. I love you.*

*Big Angelle."*

I closed the notebook up and put it back inside of my bag.

"I'm proud of you, Angelle." Shareese reached for a tissue.

"Oh, Shareese, please don't do that." I looked up at the ceiling. I could feel the tears starting to form in the corners of my eyes. She passed me a tissue, too.

"Believe me, these are tears of joy." She dabbed each eye one at a time.

"Mine are, too." I took a deep breath. "And I owe it all to you, Shareese. You really brought me back to life." We both stood up to give one another a hug. After our embrace I reached down and pick up my bag to leave.

"Angelle, don't leave just yet. Sit back down for a moment."

"Why, what's wrong, Shareese?"

"There's something else that we need to talk about," she stated. I sat back down in the chair. "I'll be right back, just give me a moment."

"What is going on?" My question was answered when Shareese returned to the room with Shantelle. "What are you doing here, Shantelle?"

"Have a seat beside your mother."

"Is everything alright? Is it Rochelle? Is Boom-Boom okay?" I asked my daughter.

"Yeah, Ma, they're alright."

"Now Angelle, I don't want you to feel ambushed in anyway. I just thought it was time for me to combine your sessions."

"Combine our sessions? What do you mean combine our sessions?"

"I have been meeting with Shantelle for over a year now . . ."

"Meeting with her for what? Shantelle, baby, what's going on?" I could feel the anxiety start to rise. "Shantelle, you're not . . ." I looked at Shareese and then back to Shantelle. "You're not pregnant are you?"

"No, Ma, of course not."

"Well, what is all of this about?" I looked up when I saw the door open again.

"Come on in Rochelle, and thank you for coming. You can sit down over there next to your family."

"Where is Boom-Boom?" I stood up and put my hands on my hips. "Will somebody please tell me what the hell is going on?"

"Angelle, the girls have something that they need to tell you and I must be honest with you, it's very disturbing. I thought it best that they tell you in this kind of setting, but just know that together we're going to get through this. Please sit down."

"What was it you said about not feeling ambushed?" I waved my arms up in the air. "What is this some kind of intervention to let me know what a terrible mother I've been to my children?"

"Ma, no. You've been a good mother to us. Why would you ever think that you haven't?"

"Angelle, I just want you to listen to what the girls have to tell you. Can you do that for me please?"

"Go ahead." I sat back down. "I'm listening." I could see that Rochelle was nervous as she sat beside me.

"Rochelle, are you ready?" Shareese asked her.

"I don't know." She started to cry. "I don't think I can." I took her hand into mine.

"Rochelle, baby, will you please tell me what's going on. I told you, you can come to me with anything. If you're pregnant again . . ."

"I'm not pregnant, Ma, I told you that," she wined.

"Well, then what it is?" I asked her, and pulled her closer to me. "Shantelle, what's wrong? Can somebody please tell me what is going on before I have a heart attack?"

"You want me to tell her for you, Rochelle?" Shantelle asked. Rochelle shook her head yes, and then buried her face in my chest. Shantelle looked at Shareese.

"It's okay," Shareese told her.

"One day I came home after working in the shop with you and daddy was . . . daddy umm . . . he was umm . . . he . . . he," she looked down.

"He what?" I looked at Shantelle who had begun to cry, too. "Tell me baby, what did he do?"

"He raped Rochelle."

"What?" I looked at Shantelle in horror. Surely I had misunderstood what she had said. Rochelle got up and ran out of the room.

"Angelle, I know this wasn't easy for you to hear, and it's a lot to process . . ."

"Did you say that your father raped Rochelle?"

"Daddy told us if we ever said anything that he would kill you before he went back to prison. He said he would kill all of us," Shantelle cried.

"Oh, my God. Lord, give me strength." Shareese came over and sat beside me. "He raped her?" I looked at Shareese. "Her own father?"

"I'm sorry Angelle, but he did," she answered in a somber tone.

"Shantelle, when did this happen?" I felt like my heart was going to jump out of my body it was beating so fast.

"Right before he died," Shantelle answered, still crying.

"Boom-Boom?" I sat all the way up in the chair. "Your daddy isn't . . . he . . . he isn't his . . . oh, my God."

# Over Before We Started!

"Pudding, somebody's at the door for you." Ma Pearl knocked on my bedroom door.

I knew Kahari would eventually show up at my house unannounced since I have been ignoring his phone calls and text messages. I don't have shit to say to him.

"I'm busy."

"Pudding, come on out of that bedroom and stop being silly."

I knew I was going to have to face him sooner or later so it might as well be tonight.

"Well, hey there, Black Stallion," I said to Kahari, after opening the door.

"Janea, I'm sorry." He closed the door. I sat back down on the bed. "I'm gon' be dead ass real with you. I used to strip, but I don't anymore."

"Umph! Shitting me." I rolled my eyes at him. "That won't you up in there shaking your ass for all to see the other night?"

"Look, one of my boys called me up at the last minute and asked me to do him a favor because he had an emergency and didn't want to cancel. I promise you, that was my last time." He sat down on the bed next to me. I scooted over to the other side.

"You talked so much about honesty and truth and look at you." I looked him up and down. "Even though no one else knew who you were, I was fucking humiliated!"

"I'm sorry Janea. I never meant to hurt you. If I'd of told you that I use to strip on the side at one time, you would have never given me a chance."

"How do you know what I would have done? I don't judge people."

"I'm sorry, baby, truly I am. I promise you I'll never do again," he pleaded.

"You don't have to promise me shit. Now that I think about it, you didn't lie to me. You told me that you were in the entertainment industry. Getting butt ball naked is very entertaining, so continue to do what you do."

"So, that's it? Just like that, it's over between us?"

"We we're over before we started. Now please leave." Kahari looked at me for a hard second, and then he got up and left out my bedroom.

My cell phone started to vibrate, and when I reached over and grabbed it off of the nightstand, I saw that it was Angelle calling me.

"What's up Angelle?"

"Hey, what are you doing?"

"Why you sound like that?"

"Like what?"

"Like you are high!"

"I am." She giggled. "Very high. I feel like I'm floating on a cloud."

"Angelle, have you been smoking weed? The last time you smoked that shit you called me sounding just like you do now." I was immediately growing frustrated with our conversation.

"No. I haven't been smoking weed," she answered still speaking in a whispered tone.

"What's up, Angelle? I'm kind of busy right now," I lied.

"Nothing, Janea, I just wanted to tell you how much I love you," she answered.

"How much you love me? Where did that come from?"

"We don't tell the people we love how much we really love them until it's too late, so I'm calling everybody to tell them . . . to tell them . . ."

"Angelle?" I called her name when the phone went silent. "Angelle, are you still there?"

"Yeah, I'm here, but not for too much longer. In a little while all my pain will be gone away. All of my struggles will be over."

The phone went silent again.

"What are you talking about, Angelle? Hello?" I looked at the phone to make sure our call was still connected. "Angelle?"

"Hmmm . . ."

"What's wrong, Angelle? Did you and Rochelle get into it again?"

"Hmmm . . ."

"Angelle?"

"I love you, Janea . . . can you promise me something?"

"Promise you what?"

"If something happens to me will you make sure my girls and Boom-Boom are okay?"

"What do I need to do that for? You'll be here to make sure they're alright. Right?" she didn't respond. "Angelle?" I looked at the phone again and we were no longer connected. *'Oh my God, she's trying to kill herself.'* I hopped up and put on my shoes, grabbed my car keys, and ran out of my bedroom with my cell phone in my other hand. "I'll be back Ma Pearl."

Angelle left her notebook at the shop one day. I read it, but I never said anything to her about what she wrote.

"9-1-1, what's your emergency?"

"I need and ambulance at 4530 Lantana Place, in Virginia Beach."

"Is this the location you're calling from?"

"No, but I'm on my way there now?" I started up my car and quickly put it into reverse.

"What's the emergency, ma'am?"

"I think someone there may be trying to commit suicide."

"What number are you calling from ma'am?"

"This is my cell phone number, now will you stop asking me all these mothafuckin' questions and send an ambulance to that address before it's too late!" I tossed my cell phone into the passenger seat and then it crossed my mind to try and call Angelle back again. I attempted several times but I only got her voice mail. "Damn you, Angelle, don't you do this shit!"

I weaved in and out of traffic and even ran the red lights to get to Angelle's house as fast as I could. She only lived about fifteen minutes away from me, but I made it to her house within ten. When I turned onto her street I was expecting to see the ambulance in the drive-way because I heard them as I was coming down the street, but the only car parked in the drive-way was Angelle's car. I flung my car in park and got out as fast as I could. I banged on the front door, but it was locked.

"Rochelle?" I called her name as I banged on the door. "Shantelle? Somebody open the door!" I wasn't about to wait for the ambulance to come and force their way into the house. It may be too late by then. I looked around the porch for something I could use to smash the window and picked up the first thing I saw—a brick! I shattered the living room window and climbed inside. The ambulance had just pulled up, so I unlocked the front door, and then I charged up the stairs. "Angelle?" I called out to her as I banged on her bedroom door. The paramedic told me to move out of the way, and then he kicked the door of the hinges. I followed him into Angelle's bedroom. "Oh, my God. No . . . no . . . no!"

# My Precious Baby!

"Now you look like my Sabrina." I spun the chair around. "Now come on over here and let me do something to them eyebrows, bitch."

"What's wrong with my eyebrows?" She turned and faced the mirror.

"They need to be cleaned up just a tad bit," I told her. "You see that's another reason why you need to bring yo' ass back home to Virginia 'cause them jealous bitches in ATL don't know how to do no damn hair for real." Sabrina started laughing.

"I like Atlanta, Juju," she said as she leaned her head back. "Virginia will always be my home, but I don't plan on coming back here to live anytime soon."

"If you say so," I rolled my eyes. "Have you seen Stephanie since you've been home?"

"No . . . owww . . . Juju, that shit hurts!" She opened her eyes. "Do you have to use tweezers to arch my eyebrows? Can't you just use the wax?"

"Beauty cost, bitch! Now hold still, I'm almost finished. So, you and your sister are still not speaking to each other?" I reached over and grabbed the alcohol.

"Juju, I told you I have given up on having a relationship with Stephanie. If you could've seen the look on her face when she told me that I was adopted that night in my momma's kitchen, you and everybody else would agree with me to just leave her ass be. Are you finished?" She sat up in the chair.

"Yeah, bitch. Get up out my chair with your worrisome ass." I unhooked the cape from around her neck. "Well, you know Stephanie been on that bullshit ever since she married that white boy."

"They do look better, Juju," Sabrina said as she examined her eyebrows through a hand mirror. "But, yeah . . . Stephanie did change after she married Kevin, but she has treated me like shit since we were little. To tell you the truth I don't even care anymore."

"Where you headed now?" I sat down at Janea's station and crossed my legs.

"I'm getting ready to go pick up Saysha from Milk's house."

"Oh, really?" I smiled "You want me to ride with you?"

"For what, so you can see Milk?" she teased me.

"Oh, heavens no." I waved my wrist in the air. "I'm over that schoolboy crush I had on Milk, but that light-skinned, Al Pacino looking brother of his looks good to me!" I popped my lips.

"Rell doesn't look like Al Pacino."

"Yes, he does honey, with that scar on the side of his face. Reminds me of Al when he played in Scarface, with his sexy ass!"

"I'mma' tell Mike you checking for another nigga." Sabrina pointed at me.

"There's nothing wrong with looking. Besides, if Mike likes it then he need to put a ring on it." I pointed to my index finger. "That's why Whitney has my last name and not his. Bitch, if you don't want me to go that's all you had to say." I rolled my neck.

"It's not like I'm going over to Milk's house to visit with him. I'm just picking up my daughter and then I'm going to my momma's house," she clarified.

"Bitch, tell me tomorrow! Don't act like it's all about Saysha. That's why you came here to get yo' hair did first. I told you before you don't have to front with me. I know you still have feelings for Milk, Sabrina."

"Juju, I'm going to always have feelings for Milk in some way or another. Look how long we were together. Plus, he's the father of my child. I have to deal with him on some level. I meant to tell you, too, I like those shoes you rocking. Where you get them from?"

"Bakers." I swung my legs around. "They fierce ain't they . . . what a minute bitch don't be trying to change the subject either. Now just go back to Atlanta, pack up yo' little shit, and bring yo' ass back home to yo' man were you belong."

"Make your damn mind up cousin." She crossed her legs to mock me. "One minute you're telling me to leave Milk's ass alone and now you're trying to put us back together. Which one is it?"

"Oh, you do such a poor imitation of me." I stood up and strolled across the room to get my purse. "I've just seen a different side of Milk since he has been bringing Ms. Diva up here to get her hair done. He's really good with the kids, Sabrina. I have to give him that."

"I agree. Milk, is an excellent father. He just sucks as a boyfriend and he sucks even worse as a husband."

"Maybe he's changed, Sabrina. I hear he's doing really well with the clubs. He owns two of them now don't he?" I put my purse on my shoulder.

"So I've heard." She made a disapproving face. "I don't ask Milk about his business, because I don't want him in mines. As long as he doesn't have my daughter around none of them skanky bitches from his club when she comes to visit him I could care less."

"He still ain't heard from that jealous bitch, Nicole?"

"Not that I know of." She stood up. I walked back over to my station to make sure I had turned off my stove. "Mj is better off without Nicole in his life. I feel sorry for him that he has to grow up without a mother, but she never wanted him in the first place and it showed. Let me borrow that MCM bag, Juju."

"The hell you say!" I looked at Sabrina as if she had insulted me. "This purse cost me two grand," I informed her. "See if you were still with Milk, you'd have three or four of these bitches right now, darling."

"Ha . . . ha . . . very funny. What are you doing tonight?"

"Not a damn thing." I turned off the lights in the front of the shop. "After a long day of perms, weaves, sew-ins, and arches, a bitch is truly tired. Whitney, come on honey, it's time to go. Mommy doesn't have time to play hide-and-seek with you. Come on out so we can go home."

"Isn't that cute, Juju is a baby momma."

"Go to hell, bitch." I walked behind her toward the front door.

"I'll call you tomorrow."

"No, I'll call you! Plus, one of them jealous bitch queens stole my damn cell phone the other night at the show, and I'm waiting for slow ass Sprint to send me another one."

"What show, Juju?"

"I'll tell you about it some other time. I'm ready to go, tootles." I waved and closed the door. "Whitney?" I walked back toward the backroom. I looked under the couch, in kitchen area, and when I still didn't see her, I walked back to the front of the shop to see if she was tucked away underneath one of the stations.

"Whitney Elizabeth Wright, you come out here this instance!" I tapped my foot on the floor. I walked back toward the backroom when she didn't appear and I noticed the back door was open. "Now who in the hell left the door open, Whitney?" I called out to her once again. "Whitney is you out here?" I walked outside and looked around but there were no signs of her. "Oh, my goodness." I frantically looked all around the empty parking lot. "I'm going to cuss somebody's ass out for free tomorrow! Who in the hell left this damn back door open?"

"Lose something?" I almost jumped out of my skin.

"Oh shit, Kunta, you scared me!" I put my hands on my chest. "And what the hell are you doing with Whitney? I have been looking all over for her. Give her to me please I don't know where your hands have been." I reached out to Kabo for him to pass Whitney to me, but he now had my precious baby dangling in the air by her coat. "Don't pick her up like that you're going to hurt her!" I hollered.

"Naw, this ain't gon' hurt her." He turned Whitney around. "But this will!"

Before I could reach Whitney, Kabo threw her down on ground and was now kicking as if she were a soccer ball.

"Mothafucka', have you lost yo' damn mind!" I screamed and charged toward him. "Stop kicking her like that Kabo, you're going to kill her!" I threw punch after punch to Kabo's head trying to stop his attack on Whitney until he flung me over his shoulders, and now I was on the ground next to Whitney. I quickly rolled over on top of her to shield her from Kabo's blows. "Why are you doing this?" I screamed. "What has she ever done to you? Oh, my God! Somebody help me!"

"Ain't nobody gon' help yo' faggot ass," he said through clenched teeth. "You 'bout to be a dead bitch just like yo' fucking mutt! You gon' wish you never told Katora where I lived, you punk mothafucka!"

"What are you talking about? I didn't tell Katora shit!" I looked down at Whitney. "Oh, my God." I started crying. "You killed her! She's dead . . . oh my God, you killed my baby," I bellowed. "I didn't tell Katora where you lived, I swear!" Kabo cuffed me by my collar. I desperately shook my head when I saw him position his fist to hit me with it. "I swear I didn't. I swear." And then it came to me. "Katora must've stolen my cell phone and got your address."

"Naw, mothafucka' talk all that slick shit now!" He punched me in the face.

"I swear, I didn't do . . ."

I tried to get up and run, but Kabo pulled me back down to the ground. I then felt another blow to my head, instantly followed by another punch . . . then another . . . and another . . . and after a few more punches, everything went black.

# Cut N' Up Too

# Coming 2013

Made in the USA
Monee, IL
24 April 2023

32341843R00144